W9-BNM-615

9.58

UNNATURALS
ESCAPE FROM LION'S HEAD

DEVON HUGHES

Illustrated by
Owen Richardson

KATHERINE **T**EGEN **B**OOKS
An Imprint of HarperCollins Publishers

Katherine Tegen Books is an imprint of HarperCollins Publishers.

ISBN 978-0-06-225757-4

17 18 19 20 21 CG/LSCH 10 9 8 7 6 5 4 3 2 1
❖
First Edition

For my mother, who loves foxes

PROLOGUE

*You often end up back where you started. That's
how it is this time: back to the beginning, to darkness, when you were so brand new your eyes
wouldn't yet open.*

*Sight is not the most important thing,
though—you learn that early.*

*Your voice is strong. You call out and the
sound bounces off the small cube of the nest, the
high walls of the space beyond it, and the creatures that move in between, looping back to you.
That first echo is how you start to understand the
world and your place in it.*

*You feel others around you, others like you.
Brothers, sisters, with leathery wings and fuzzy
bodies. They wriggle against you. Small wet noses
nuzzle your ears, and bushy tails cradle your
head.*

You can hear them well enough, too. They

wake up crying out, "mother" and "hungry," and their squeaking voices sound like your own.

Mother doesn't come, but something else does. Someone.

His feet make squeaking sounds as he approaches, but they don't sound like your squeaks, and the rhythm tells you he has two feet instead of four. His scent is strong and unnatural. He picks you up in a paw that has five long digits, squeezing the fine bones of your wings together, and he places a hard nozzle in your mouth.

The powdery milk fills you up.

"You're special," he tells you, placing you back in the nest. "You're going to change everything."

You feel happy and heavy with the sweet milk, and you believe him.

"Hello," you tell the world. The echo of your voice tells you that you are safe from prey, and that there are others close by to protect you, and you trust it.

You nestle down into the warmth of the nest, your heart beating in quick time with your littermates' as you drift off to sleep.

PART ONE

FREE
AS A
BIRD

"Deeper Cuts in Food and Housing; Citizens Escape into Virtual Reality"

"Can Underdog Save Team Scratch from Invincible's Wrath?"

"Matchmaker Joni Juniper Announces Surprise Resignation"

THE CREATURE OPENED HER EYES AND WAS NEARLY BLINDED by the bright light. *Still daytime.*

She hugged her gray wings tighter around her body and shrank back into their darkness, trying to hold on to the dream—if you could call it that. She was never sure if it was dream or memory or just a story she told herself. Whether she'd really even been asleep.

"I've gotta split," one of the humans announced. The creature recognized the voice. It was Vince, the trainer.

The creature poked her head out. More than a hundred feet below her, the other mutant animals were back inside their cages, and the humans were packing up the lab, disinfecting the harnesses, swabs, and tools. Today's trials were already over.

The creature breathed a sigh of relief. So she had slept for most of the day, after all.

"Keep an eye on my Kill Clan," Vince called over his shoulder to one of the six researchers. They all dressed in crinkly yellow from head to toe and wore paper masks over their faces, so the creature couldn't tell them apart.

"Lazy Draino," whispered one of the Yellow Six, an older man. Thanks to her large, triangular ears, the creature had excellent hearing.

"He's just going to the bookies to gamble on tomorrow's big Unnaturals match," another human in yellow, this one a woman, answered.

The creature noticed that although the researchers always grumbled about Vince after he'd gone, they didn't say these things when he was around. She also noticed that Vince was the only one who could control the animals after they became mutants. Each group seemed to be getting more violent than the last.

"Are you going to watch it?" the man asked, coiling

up the breathing tube they used to test lung capacity. "The Underdog versus the Invincible?"

"No, but my kids will warp into the match, I'm sure. They're major Moniacs. My daughter really likes that eagle-dog."

"Doesn't have much of a chance, does he? Remember what happened last season? If they're just going to let the scorpion-tiger destroy all the other mutants, what's the point?" Only his eyes were visible above the mask, and the glasses he wore reflected the light like mirrors. To the creature, the man looked like a fat yellow fly.

"Hey, those ticket sales pay for our research." The woman held up a glass tube and shook it. "And it's not like we haven't seen worse in here."

They glanced toward the far end of the space, where a chain-link fence ran the length of the room. No longer useful, the mutants that had already failed the genetic tests mingled freely on the other side. The fence clinked and bulged as bodies pressed against it. They always got restless after Vince left.

"We should get going," the woman in yellow said nervously. They were the last two of the Yellow Six left. The man collected his jar of samples and hurried out after her, clicking off the lights on his way out the door.

Their day of work had ended, but the creature's was just beginning. She had a long night of hunting ahead of her.

She shook the stiffness out of her wings and the sleep out of her eyes, and then she clenched her toes on the metal slats of the vent to swing herself back upright. From her high perch, she surveyed the room below, wondering where to start. Since she rarely let herself be seen during the day, the creature had to gather everything that would sustain her under the cloak of darkness.

The other animals were still settling down, so first she crept to the corners of the room to check the traps she had set for wayward mice. Finding nothing there, she trotted over between the rows of stacked cages, her four legs making long, swift strides as she stalked her prey. Spotting the dart of a shadow, the creature pounced!

Her paws landed squarely on the fattest, juiciest cockroach she had ever seen. Dinner was served. She let out a little screech of happiness, but the way it echoed back to her ears sounded strangely flat, and instead of chowing down on the roach, she paused, looking at the empty cage in front of her.

That was where the panda had been—the one the Yellow Six called Mai. They must've finally taken her for the injection today.

4

The creature didn't usually get to know the new animals. They rarely stayed in the individual cages long before they were turned into mutants and moved to the other side of the fence in the group pen, dazed and bloodthirsty. And besides, she was different from them—she was nighttime, while they were daytime; she soared in the rafters, while they cowered in cages—and she preferred to keep her distance.

But the panda had lasted through eight versions of the serum without being pulled for testing. The Six seemed to like her. They were always cooing over her big, fluffy head and her perfect round ears and her curious, coal-rimmed eyes.

The creature just thought Mai's eyes looked sad. And sometimes at night, the creature would hear Mai singing songs to herself in the darkness, and those sounded sad, too. The creature avoided the area near the cages when the caged bear sang, letting the cockroaches skitter by unchecked.

Now, the creature looked down at her front paws and realized the juicy king cockroach had gotten away, too. In her surprise about Mai, she must've relaxed her grip.

Maybe the serum was successful this time, she thought hopefully, as she unfolded her wings and took to the air. *Maybe it did whatever Bruce and the Yellow Six hoped it would do, instead of turning sweet Mai into a snarling, red-eyed monster.* But as the creature swooped down to feast on the flies that buzzed above the warm, sleeping bodies, she heard a commotion on the other side of the lab.

There was growling and frenzied movement behind the fence, and the creature heard Mai's voice, no longer musical. It was changed by madness, or changed by pain. She would be something new, with wings or horns or scales. The creature knew that the herd in the group pen often turned on new additions and hoped that wouldn't happen to Mai.

Sometimes, when Vince arrived in the early mornings to train his "Clan," the creature saw him removing injured animals from the pen after he changed the water.

The creature didn't want to see him dragging out Mai's body. She didn't want to see the Yellow Six coaxing other frightened animals from their cages and snapping them into the harnesses to run their trials. She didn't want to see Bruce, and hear the *click click* of his pen after each injection, when he'd write down what happened.

This time, she especially didn't want to see What Happened.

She had a while yet before she'd hear the buzz of the

overhead lights on their timers announcing the humans' coming arrival. She could still get some good hunting in.

But the creature had lost her appetite, and she already felt exhausted.

She flapped her wings and watched the space between herself and the other mutants grow, until what she had thought was a bear footprint now looked like nothing more than a shadow on the floor. The creature retreated back into her high perch, out of sight.

The creature hooked her feet into the vent in the ceiling to hang upside down. The rush of blood to her head was instantly calming, and she sighed. She clutched her tawny orange tail to her chest for its soft comfort, and wrapped her wings around herself, shutting out the world. Flexing her toes to make her body sway, the creature was beginning to rock herself back into a familiar dream.

And that's when the room exploded.

2

PERHAPS THE ROOM HAD NOT ACTUALLY EXPLODED. BUT that was certainly how it felt. There was a terrible sound, and then the creature felt the crack vibrate up the walls and through her body.

She poked her head out of the tent of her wings to see what was going on below. She thought it must be the humans, trying out some new test, but the walkway outside the door was still silent, the lab still dark. Below her, the docile animals were milling around their cages with dazed expressions. Across the room, she could see the agitation of the more violent mutants as bits of plaster rained down around them. The explosion had come from behind the fence.

The creature followed the dust storm and discovered a fresh hole in the wall—a wall that, until this moment, had seemed as constant and indestructible as the humans. Out of the hole slithered a snake, its scales covered in the white powder.

The snake coiled herself up, her diamond-shaped head lifting to take in her surroundings. When she saw the other mutants, the snake froze.

The other animals froze, too, but an almost imperceptible shiver went through them, and even without seeing them, the creature knew that their pupils were dilating.

The creature thought of the reaction as the "kill drive," and she had seen it activated many times. It usually happened during research trials with the Yellow Six, or else in one-on-one fights Vince set up in the smaller pen when he needed to make room for new mutants. They were probably still hyped up from attacking Mai.

The creature couldn't remember how she'd escaped from Bruce and the Yellow Six, but she knew she didn't have the kill drive, or the indifference to pain that went

9

with it. That's why she lived most of her life alone, high up in these rafters, keeping far away from everyone.

She would not want to be in the snake's position right now.

Sensing the danger she was in, the snake shot away from the other animals. She was quick and skilled at slithering between their feet, but there were many, many mutants, and soon she was backed into a corner against the fence, her tongue flicking and her tail rattling as they advanced on her with herky-jerky movements.

At least it would be over quickly.

But just as her attackers started to hurl themselves at her, two hidden slits opened on the snake's back, and a pair of wings snapped out between the scales. In the next instant, the snake took flight.

Other than herself, the creature had never seen another mutant fly. Many of them had wings, but they were too dazed, or too restricted, or too sick to use them. The creature's wings were made of thin, gray skin stretched out over tiny bones. They were flexible and scalloped on the bottom, allowing her to maneuver easily through the air. The snake's wings were different—rounded and delicate, with swirling patterns—like some of the insects the creature caught at night.

And like those moths she hunted, the flying snake

seemed to be attracted to the overhead lights, even though they were dimmed. The snake floated up and up, and the creature was too mesmerized to realize it was headed right for her!

"Hey! How do I get out?" the snake demanded, suddenly face-to-face.

"What?" gasped the creature, still upside down, peering out fearfully over her wrapped wings.

Despite being in a room with hundreds of other mutants, no one ever talked to her—she wasn't sure most of them *could* talk—and she spent most of her waking hours in darkness, alone. Now, this new animal was not only speaking to her, but it was asking her something that didn't make any sense. And it was not asking very nicely.

"Out!" the snake repeated. "I know you can't be deaf with those big ears. Where's-s-s the way outside?"

The creature had no idea what this strange snake was hissing about, but it was pressing closer and closer to her, and the creature felt too frightened to take flight.

"I don't want to hurt you. But I will." The snake's eyes were a light milky gray, like hard glass. "All I want is to get home."

Home?

It was a human word. That was where the Yellow

Six talked about going at night. She couldn't understand why anyone would want go where they were. But the snake was baring her fangs and rattling her tail now, and the creature knew if she didn't answer soon, something very bad was going to happen—if not with the snake, then with the humans. The lights would be clicking on any minute now, and when Vince arrived and saw the snake, the creature would be discovered, too.

"The humans go through those two doors," the creature answered finally, gathering her courage. "There." She pointed one of her white-tipped paws down toward the EXIT sign. "And there." She gestured across the room, to the door marked *H*.

The snake's diamond-shaped head was already zigzagging in dissent. "I don't care where the humans go. Everyone knows humans don't go into the s-s-sun," she hissed. "I mean the way *outside*. A tunnel through the walls. To the desert. Or the Greenplains-s-s."

Greenwhat? The creature's world was white walls and steel cages. The brightest color she'd encountered was the yellow of the scientists' suits.

"The only tunnel I've seen is the one you made. I, um, don't think that there *is* a way out."

"WHAT?" the snake shouted the word so loudly that her jaws unhinged. "There has-s-s to be. Moss's

12

stories-s-s about escaped Unnaturals, Castor's babble about freedom . . . it can't all end here in another lab."

The overhead lights switched on, one by one, casting a pale, greenish glow over the room.

"They're coming," the creature warned. "You should go back to where you came from—wherever that is."

"Back to NuFormz?" the snake scoffed, glancing at the hole she'd slithered out of. "Back to prison, to fighting for human enjoyment, to a dumb eagle-dog talking nonsense about teamwork, when my team never cared a lick about me? Never."

Teamwork. The unfamiliar idea echoed in the creature's ears. "It must be better than here," she murmured.

Turning away, the snake careened around the ceiling, her moth wings fluttering erratically as she flung herself into the far corners of the room and veered too close to the fans. The creature was grateful that the snake would be preoccupied far away from her when the humans came.

Of course, now the snake was zooming back toward her. The creature saw the flick of forked tongue and the flash of fang and winced, preparing for the snake's venomous strike. Instead, the snake looked past her with narrowed eyes.

"That. There."

The vent? The one she hung from each time she went to sleep?

"It blows cool air," the creature started to explain, but the snake shoved her aside.

The creature heard the skitter of tiny paws and realized the snake must've spotted one of the mice that lived on the other side. Was the snake planning to hunt now? It didn't seem like the best time.

The creature watched in horror as the snake began to smash her body against the vent. *Bang! Bang!* There was a dent, and then a screw came loose, and then the edge started to come away from the wall . . .

And then came the sound of a key jiggling in the lock.

Humans.

Hearing two sets of boots instead of one, the creature knew that the other man, Horace, must be with Vince. That meant they'd brought a new animal today.

The metal door swung open, and sure enough, Horace tromped in, round and red-faced, and Vince's smaller, muscled body followed. They carried a cage down the walkway, its weight swaying between them.

The creature's eyesight was poor, especially in daylight, so she couldn't see what was inside the cage. But the snake saw—she got a clear view of whatever was in

14

that cage before the men were even aware she was in the room.

"It looks like Castor, my old enemy," the snake hissed with recognition, more to herself than the creature. "Like the shepherd dog before the mutation."

Moments ago, the snake's face had been full of desperation. Now, as the creature watched, that expression changed. While it didn't quite look like the kill drive—there was no foam coming from the snake's mouth—there was definitely murder in her eyes. Her long body began to twitch, and the rattle made a *shhhhhh* that hushed the room.

A shiver traveled down the creature's spine and every mutant on the floor looked up. Soon the men would notice, too. The creature shrank back into the shadows in fear, but the flying snake paid no attention to the humans. Instead, all of her frustration and rage at not being able to find a way outside was redirected at the animal in the cage.

"This is for your brother," she shouted down. "For the stupid Underdog and his lies-s-s-s-s-s!"

Then, abandoning all hope, the snake turned away from both the creature and the vent, tucked her wings in, and dove at the cage.

3

VINCE AND HORACE DIDN'T NOTICE THE DIVE-BOMBING snake until she was almost upon them.

The creature let out an accidental screech in anticipation of the impact, and both men looked up suddenly, squinting against the bright lights.

"What the—?" Vince gasped.

Horace's thick black eyebrows shot up his forehead in surprise. "How'd she get loose?"

The creature shrank back behind a ceiling beam. Had they seen her?

That's all either of them had time to say, though. Then there was a terrific crash as the snake hit the cage head-on.

The cage flew out of the men's hands, somersaulting through the air. It clattered to the floor at the far side of the room, and upon impact, the door sprang open on its hinges, and the animal inside tumbled out.

The creature peered around the beam. She saw a thin, mangy-looking dog lying still on the linoleum in front of the fence.

Back near the entrance, the butterfly-snake lay limp near the dented cage, with a long gash on her head tearing some of her glossy scales. Her delicate wings were now torn and ragged.

For a few long seconds, Vince, Horace, and both freed animals seemed too stunned to move. Then the door opened for the Yellow Six to file in with their supplies, and the whole room sprang to life.

Vince's Kill Clan mutants began flinging themselves against the metal fence in a frenzy, trying to get at the new animal on the other side.

The injured snake darted between Vince's legs to

slither toward the dog, who was still sprawled on the floor.

Both men reached for their pockets to retrieve golden whistles.

The creature blacked out for half a second at the trill of the whistles—she had sensitive hearing, anyway, and the sound was so high-pitched that it was physically painful—but when she came to, the dog, roused by the whistle, was bounding toward the open door, the snake trailing close behind.

Horace reached out a meaty hand and caught the dog by the scruff of its neck, but the snake didn't stop. She didn't seem to be aware of her shredded wings, the cut on her head, or even the men. Focused on her prey, she opened her jaws wide, as if she were preparing to swallow the poor dog whole.

Just before she struck, Vince swiped a syringe dart of mutating serum from one of the scientists' trays and flung it toward the trio in one smooth motion. The needle disappeared between the snake's scales, and within seconds, the snake's body stiffened and she abandoned her pursuit.

Now that the excitement was over, the Yellow Six filed into the lab. Normally, the creature was asleep by the time the scientists began their rounds, and if she wasn't, she definitely had no intention of venturing anywhere near to where they were working. Normally, she tried to stay as far away from the humans as possible, not to mention the other mutants.

But today was not a normal day. This snake was special. She was from somewhere *else*—even if it was somewhere worse. The creature's curiosity outweighed her fear.

The creature unhooked her feet from the vent and flew across the ceiling, careful to stay in the shadows of the rafters. Then she crept down a pipe along one wall near the cages of untested animals.

It was still pretty safe, she reasoned. The pipe was tucked behind a supply shelf, obscured from view. The lab tables were nearby, but the Six were busy setting up their equipment for now. The newer animals around the creature were focused on remaining silent in their cages and not attracting attention, and the Kill Clan was all the way on the other side of the room, behind the fence. Looking past the scientists, the creature still had a clear sightline of the men standing near the door with the snake.

"Is that really the Cunning?" one of the Yellow Six called out.

Vince nodded, flashing his teeth. "Sure is." He

grabbed a net off a hook near the fence and scooped up the writhing, wounded serpent. "Though the butterfly-snake ain't that smart if she ended up here, if you ask me."

"No one's asking you anything," Horace grumbled, his attention divided as he struggled to hold on to the whining dog. "You just gave one of the mayor's prized Unnaturals stars an extra shot of serum—unauthorized."

"Who knows?" Vince joked. "Maybe Bruce finally got the ingredients right and she'll get a superhero upgrade. Be half human or something. Bet Mayor Eris would even give me a promotion."

"Maybe. Or maybe the snake will wind up like the others in your little Kill Clan. Worthless. You like to gamble, eh? What do you think those odds are?"

Horace shouldered past Vince, dragging the dog behind him as he headed for the cages . . . and right toward the creature!

He was sure to see her hanging here if he got much closer. The creature crept onto the shelving unit and crouched between the boxes, careful to keep her pale orange fur hidden under the shield of her wings.

The shelf wobbled a little under her weight, and the creature imagined the boxes falling, the glass tubes and microscopes shattering, and all the humans running toward her at once. But she held her breath, and the shelf settled.

Horace shoved the dog into Mai's now-empty cage, and Vince hurried behind him, carrying the net. The creature was glad to get a better look at the snake, but that also meant she was closer to the humans than she'd ever been.

She noticed that Vince had the sharp eyes of a predator, but the small, scrappy build of an animal regularly made to fight for his survival. Horace had fur on his face, hands as big as bear paws, and a stare that suggested his sting would be poisonous. The creature wouldn't want to tangle with either of them, and she was already wishing she was back in her high perch, safe in her nest.

But first she wished she could talk to the snake one more time. The serpent seemed to know so many things that the creature did not.

The things that the snake knew would soon be replaced with the familiar blankness of the rest of the Kill Clan, though. The snake wriggled and writhed, trying to escape the mesh, and the creature saw that foam was already gathering at her unhinged mouth. Her body was starting to mutate further, her scales taking on a strange glow.

"What was in the mix this time?" Vince asked one of the researchers.

"Jellyfish," a woman in yellow answered.

"What'd I say?" Horace said, gesturing at the net. "She'll probably dissolve into goo now. Worthless."

"Doesn't matter what happens to the Cunning, though, right? I mean, she wasn't on the mayor's winners list or anything." Vince's tone was light, but if there was one thing the creature knew how to spot, it was fear. "Right, Horace?" Vince pressed.

"Yeah, maybe this mutant's lucky," Horace answered finally. "The rest of 'em are bound for the Mega Monster Mash-up to get slaughtered."

"What do you mean?" Vince narrowed his eyes, confused. "*All of them?* Again? Except the Underdog, right? You always said he could be a killer in disguise."

Horace grunted noncommittally.

"Come on, Horace," Vince pressed. "Do you know how much I have riding on the Invincible vs. Underdog match tonight? You owe me some intel."

Vince was always aggressive with the animals, but with Horace, the creature saw that he could be self-conscious, too. It was like he was puffing himself up or displaying all his feathers. Testing his boundaries.

"Owe you?" Horace repeated. His red face flushed

deeper, and he clenched his thick hands into fists. "I got you this gig, didn't I? I've more than paid my debts."

The scientists eyed the arguing men and moved farther away from the cages, giving them space.

"You said it would get my people out of the Drain," Vince whispered loudly. "So far, it's just cleaning up after zombies and 'roid ragers."

Horace shrugged. "Talk to Bruce. He's working on the new serum. Until there's some progress on that, your plans will have to wait."

"There's always a new serum. Look around you. Every monster in this place is a failed experiment from one of his serums. In the meantime, give me *something*. Tell me what the Unnaturals odds are, at least."

"To get something, you gotta give something." Horace looked away, bored.

"Fine." Vince cleared his throat. "Twenty percent of my winnings. I know the mayor doesn't let you bet on the matches."

"Thirty," Horace said sharply.

"Deal. So what's the scoop?"

"The match tonight is cancelled. Eris decided to move up the championship instead—figured the people could use a fresh start. Let's just say you'd be stupid to bet on either Team Klaw or Team Scratch in the Mega Mash-up."

"But if I were a betting man? Who does the mayor want to win? There's gotta be a last monster standing, right?"

"Well, it was supposed to be the Cunning . . ." Horace glanced at the glowing snake, now lying still inside the net. "But looks like you screwed that up."

The humans had talked about these Unnaturals matches before, about a fighting ring, about placing bets on one team or another, but the creature hadn't realized they were talking about real animals outside the room until now. The snake knew about them—the snake had been one of them—but now the things the snake knew were melting away as the serum worked its way through her veins.

That was warning enough, and the creature wanted to make her way back to her nest, where she would forget about the snake and everything else outside this room. But for now, until the men left, she was trapped.

"Let's just say you *absolutely* wouldn't want to bet on the eagle-dog," Horace continued. "With your buddies in the Drain complaining about food pills and over-crowding, the mayor thought an underdog beating the odds wasn't the best message to send the ritzy sky people of Lion's Head. Word is, that flying mutt's number is up." He dragged a thick finger across his throat.

At Horace's words, there was a sudden howl from Mai's old cage. The dog had managed to stay quiet through the snake attack and everything that came after, but now he was riled up. And it seemed like he was in anguish.

"Shut up!" Horace roared, slamming a boot into the side of the cage, but it only made the dog whine louder.

"Hey, you." Vince gestured to one of the Six, who glanced at him over the yellow mask. "Gimme a syringe. We need some more of that zombie juice."

"No, you don't." Horace leaned in close to Vince's face. "You've done enough damage for one day. I've told you before, this is a *lab*, and it runs on *order*, not just pumped-up testosterone like your gangs in the Drain."

Vince clenched his jaw. It was an insult he would remember later. "You sound like that egghead Bruce."

"Yeah, well, call yourself Master of the Kill Clan all you want, but Bruce is the boss, far as we're concerned, and you don't give shots without his or the mayor's say-so."

"So what am I supposed to do with this howling mutt?"

Horace shrugged. "I look like I care?"

"You're the one who found him prowling around the Dome. Why don't you take him up to NuFormz?

If they're starting fresh, they'll need new Unnaturals recruits, right?"

Horace shook his head. "They're stopping the matches. The serums are too powerful now. The new mutants are too hard to control."

"I can control them."

Horace huffed. "Wait and see what Bruce says. Until then, he's your problem."

The dog was the creature's problem as much as Vince's. His howls continued throughout the afternoon and kept all the human's attention focused on the cages near where she hid.

Finally, late in the day, Vince announced he was moving the dog to H-Ward. The scientists' eyes shifted above their masks.

"Are you sure that's a good idea?" one asked, clearly uneasy.

"There's a treatment going on," another countered.

"Bruce is the only one who goes in the H-Ward."

"It's a stable environment, and we're not supposed to—"

"What, you all afraid of a kid?" Vince smirked. "Maybe Little Miss Sky Girl wants a friend. Anyway, I hear it's soundproof."

The scientists shook their heads and clicked their

tongues as Vince dragged the dog's cage across the room toward the door with the big *H* on it.

Now was her chance to get back to her perch, but the creature was so shaken from the day's activities that she didn't dare move from the shelf until the last human was gone from the room. She stayed crouched between the boxes of lab supplies for hours, her legs cramping up, waiting for this strange day to end.

4

THE WHITE DOOR MARKED H-WARD WAS NOT, IN FACT, soundproof. At least not for the creature. When Vince shoved the cage inside the room, the dog went right on crying, and when he closed the door behind him, he and the other humans didn't seem to hear it anymore. But thanks to the creature's sensitive hearing, the sound was only muffled a little bit. Hours passed, and the humans left, and the lights clicked off. And still, the dog howled. It was making another sound, too, a strange gargling that the creature found disturbing.

The creature was used to unwanted sounds. The room was full of many mutants, and all day, their various noises would interrupt the creature's dreams. The whir of fans was constant, the lights hummed with electricity, and music blasted through a loudspeaker, echoing around the walls. And some animal was *always* screaming for help, especially when Bruce came to visit. You couldn't let yourself be bothered by each troubling sound, or you'd never get any rest.

But all that noise happened during the day. At night, the silence was hers, and the creature needed peace to plan her traps. She needed quiet to hunt roaches.

It had been a long, exciting day, and with all the commotion, the creature hadn't gotten a wink of sleep. Now, she was so tired she could barely think, and all the creature wanted was to quickly nourish her body and collapse into her nest. Yet the dog would not quit, so tonight, it seemed she'd have to settle for some easily snagged flies.

She flew through the darkness, her strong wings and echolocation guiding her when her strained eyes could not, but she didn't sense the movement of any tasty insects. That dog's cries were even scaring off the prey!

Agitated, the creature dove down to the floor and landed at a trot, snapping her wings in as her four legs

29

padded quickly between the lab tables toward the door marked *H*.

"Hey!" she yipped. "You in there!"

The howls stopped for a moment, and the creature was startled by her own voice. She didn't speak very often, anyway, and it was strange to be standing out here in the open talking loudly, even if the other mutants were asleep behind bars.

"Listen, you need to stop all that yelling," the creature said firmly, her voice lower now. "It's not going to help you, anyway. The humans are already gone, and when they come back in the morning, the louder you howl, the faster they're going to strap you into a harness and stick you with a needle."

Now the wailing resumed at full force, practically piercing her eardrums. She felt the sound reverberate inside her teeth.

She guessed she had said the wrong thing.

The creature tried to backtrack, making soothing sounds through the door, but it didn't make any difference. He was inconsolable.

Now some of the other mutants were starting to stir in their sleep, and the creature knew that if the Kill Clan got worked up at night, there would be bodies in the morning. After Mai, after the snake, she just didn't think she could handle that right now.

The creature swiped a clamp from one of the lab tables, and clenching the pincers between her teeth, she was able to turn the doorknob. With the door open, the dog's cries were even louder, and so shrill she almost had to turn away. The creature quickly shut the door behind her before the other mutants woke up fully.

H-Ward was even darker than the Room, but there were metal posts at her eye level—more lab tables, she assumed. Anyway, she didn't need to see. She could hear the howls just fine, so she knew right where the dog was.

She crept toward the back corner, and as she neared the cage, the dog peered out at her with bright, pained eyes.

Suddenly the creature felt the fur along her spine stand up, and her flight response kicked in. What was she *doing*, approaching an unknown animal? This went against everything she had learned about how to survive in the Room!

She almost bolted right then, but now that she was close enough to see his muzzle moving, the creature could make out the dog's voice inside the howls. "Help," it begged. "Help me."

It jogged some memory in her, some piece of a dream, and she thought of a nest, and warm bodies wriggling against her, and screeches and squeaks, and she couldn't leave him.

"Shh!" she whispered. "Quiet now!"

The animal didn't have that wary look to him like most of the new ones did—the look that said he had been through this before, in one place or another. This one looked brand new. Panicky, anxious. He didn't even seem to know how to stand in the cage, and his paws kept catching on the wiry floor.

The dog's whimpering tapered off a little, as his curiosity got the better of him. "W-w-what . . . are you?"

"I do not understand."

The dog said the same thing twice more, in different, goofy accents. The creature almost laughed, despite herself. What a weird thing he was!

"I can understand the words. I mean I don't understand what you mean by them. I'm just me." The creature was what she was, nothing more.

"Well, I am a dog, you know! Ma was a German shepherd and they say my daddy was part Mexican wolf, which is why I'm so resilient, my brother says, even though I'm the littlest one and the pack doesn't take me serious and they laughed when I said I'd find him but I know I will if I can just get out!" He took a deep breath and looked away for a moment, his eyes turning sad, but then they snapped back to her and he was panting again. "Are you a dog, too?"

"I don't think so, I . . ."

He stuck his nose through the bars, inhaling her scent, and the creature backed up instinctively.

"Your legs kind of look like a dog. Maybe your face, too, with that snout." He cocked his head, considering, and one of his triangular ears flopped to the side. "It's smaller, though, almost like a cat. But your tail is so big and bushy!" He turned around in the cage, angling to get a better look.

The creature had never felt so interesting. Or so strange. For a moment, she wished she'd never left the safe haven of the rafters, where no one could see any part of her.

"I haven't seen that color before on a dog, no, not ever. It's like the sun. Or the sky when the sun lights it on fire."

"You've seen the sky?" the creature asked in surprise, but the dog kept chattering on. He talked so fast the creature could hardly keep up.

"And you have wings, too! Like Castor. Castor, that's my brother. Have you seen him? Castor has wings, but they're like a bird's. An eagle's. That's what it said on the posters. Eagle-dog. Underdog. Yours are different, though, they're black and stretchy, can I feel?"

He pawed at the bars, trying to touch her wings. The creature took another, bigger, step back.

"They're actually gray," she said, stretching her wings. "And I haven't seen a dog with wings. Just a snake."

"They told me I wouldn't find him when I left home. The pack said I was stupid, but I wouldn't listen, and now look what's happened. Maybe they were right, actually, do you think they were right?" Now the dog let out another mournful cry.

There was that word *home* again! Maybe it wasn't just where the humans went. "Where is home?" she asked the dog over his howls. "And where is outside?"

"Outside?" the dog sniffled. "It's where the sky is. And the sun."

"Outside." The creature repeated the word. She liked the feel of it in her mouth. It almost had a taste. *Something juicy*, she thought. *Filling.* "And you say you've been there?"

"Yes. Yes, of course." He perked up a little. "I am from outside. I am from the alley on the Southside of Lion's Head, near the trash mountains."

"I am from the Room," the creature replied.

The dog looked at her strangely. "What about your name, huh? My name is Runt, what's yours?"

"I . . . I don't know." The creature had never thought about having a *name* before.

"You're from this room and you don't have a name? How can you not have a name?"

She thought of Mai. Being given a name by the Yellow Six didn't seem like a good thing. It just meant they were paying attention to you, and that was the last thing the creature wanted.

But then he said, "What do your friends call you?"

The creature stared at him, confused.

"Hang on, there's a tag on your ear," the dog said, smushing his face into the bars to get a closer look. "I was learning to read from the advertisements, just like my brother Castor. Here, turn your head this way, I can't see it." His eyeball bulged as he peered at her tag and read the code aloud. "*K-07M0*. Kozmo? I think it says Kozmo." The dog called Runt grinned with satisfaction, his tongue hanging out of his mouth.

Now the creature had a name. It felt no stranger than not having one.

"Kozmo, what happens here?" Runt whispered, suddenly serious again.

At last, a question she could answer. "You will get a shot."

"And I'll be a mutant?" His eyes went round and white.

"It's not so bad," she insisted.

"Not for you. But you're different. The other ones, the ones by the fence, they look . . . rabid."

The creature was different. But she didn't quite know why.

"And why aren't you in a cage? Why am I in one? I want to get out."

For a moment, the creature thought about trying to use the human tool to pry open the cage door, but freeing a strange animal seemed like a very bad idea. How could she trust him to not attack her? Maybe it was time to leave. She set the clamp down on the floor.

"No, don't go!" he whimpered. "I'm scared of the sounds."

"What sounds?" she asked, twitching her ears. This was the first time the dog had stayed quiet for long enough for her to hear anything else but his barking. She realized there were machines in the room with them. The whirs and beeps were so much a part of the creature's normal life that she barely registered them, but for the dog, they must have seemed frightening. "That's just lab equipment. Nothing to be afraid of."

"What about something watching me?"

The creature felt that way, too, sometimes—like there were eyes on her, even in the darkness.

"You don't have to worry about that right now, either. The humans are gone until morning."

"Please don't leave me alone." He whined, and she was afraid he might start howling again.

No one had ever asked the creature for anything, and she was surprised to find that she wanted to stay, to comfort the dog. She had all night to hunt, after all. She could stay for a little while—at least until he fell asleep.

She knew this was foolish, of course. There was no use worrying about other creatures—especially weak, doomed creatures such as this one. Soon Bruce would give him the shot, and he would be like all the rest: deranged, dazed, pliable. No matter what type of animal they were, with horns or hooves or spots or stripes, the serum gave them all the same vacant eyes, the same blood set to boil.

All except her.

But foolish or not, the creature curled up next to his cage. She liked how warm it felt to lie next to someone. She even pushed her bushy tail through the bars so that Runt could rest his head on it. It made her imagine that she had a different sort of life—one *outside*, one with a home. At least now she had a name.

Kozmo, she thought to herself. *It's what your friends call you.*

5

Kozmo woke to the muffled sound of human voices. Not only had she missed the best hours for hunting, but she had also missed the click of the lights and the commotion of waking mutants. She had been so tired that she'd slept through the whole night. Any other time, safe on her perch, losing a night to catch up on sleep wouldn't have been such a big deal. But this night, she wasn't safe on her perch. She was still huddled next to the dog's cage—inside a forbidden room!

Hearing a gurgling across the room, Kozmo leapt to her feet, bumping into Runt's cage and rattling the metal bars as she did so. The dog didn't budge. He was lying with his belly up and tongue out, yipping softly, still safe inside some happy dream.

Meanwhile, Kozmo was living a nightmare.

Now that the lights were on, Kozmo could see that there weren't more lab tables in this room, as she'd thought last night. Instead, beds lined the walls. They had lots of fancy straps and gadgets attached to them. All twenty beds were empty—except one.

In the middle bed on one wall, a human girl lay sprawled out on the soft padding. Dozens of stickers were suctioned to her body, and the wires attached to them fed into one of the machines. A thick coat of blue goo had been spread over her arms, and the substance sizzled and bubbled in places. The tube shoved into her mouth appeared to be the cause of the gurgling. Her face was so pale and dry, it blended in with her paper gown, and her unsettling brown eyes stared out of hollow sockets. The researchers were treating their test subject as if she was some kind of toy!

Kozmo had thought a shot of serum was the most awful thing that could happen, but whatever the Yellow Six were doing to this girl, it was worse.

When she noticed Kozmo looking at her, the girl started to gurgle louder, making desperate groans. The machine next to the bed let out a series of beeps. Surely someone would be coming in soon to check on it.

"Runt!" Kozmo whispered urgently. She nudged the cage harder. "Wake up!"

"Hmm?" the dog murmured, still half dreaming.

The tip of his tail was sticking out of the bars of the cage, and Kozmo nibbled it with her pointy incisors. That got his attention.

"YOW!" he barked, fully awake now. "What did you do that for?"

"There's something else in here with us," Kozmo squeaked. "Look!"

"Oh, her," Runt said with a yawn, arching his back for a stretch.

"You *knew* she was in here?" Kozmo couldn't believe what she was hearing.

"I told you she was watching me. Eyes following everything I did, rolling, rolling around. Creepy, huh? And the gurgles. Yikes. Lucky for me you stayed, huh!"

Lucky for Runt, but not so lucky for Kozmo.

"I should have left sooner," she despaired. "The humans are already in the lab. How am I going to sneak past them now? And what if she tells on us?"

Runt looked at the girl on the bed. "Stop that gurgling!" he barked. "You're making Kozmo very nervous!"

"Shh!" Kozmo snapped.

Runt shut his mouth for the first time and looked at her with wide eyes. "I think she's actually quite friendly," he whispered.

Had the people heard them? Luckily, their ears were too weak to hear the commotion through the door. Still, Kozmo could hear them just fine. Their voices were clearer now. *Close.*

"Antonio, what'd I say about trailing me when I'm working?"

Kozmo recognized Vince's voice right away. It had an edge to it this morning, an irritation that he rarely expressed with the animals, and certainly not with Horace.

"Sorry, V. It's just that I need help. I . . . I need a truck."

Kozmo didn't know the second voice, but it sounded a lot like Vince's. It was in the same tonal range, just a bit higher and with some weird cracks in the middle of words.

Vince burst into laughter. "A truck? Bro, you're thirteen! What do *you* need wheels for?"

"It's actually for Leesa."

"Oh, man, you got it bad for her, huh?" Now Vince's

41

voice was lilting cheerfully. "You want me to give you a loaner so you can take your little princess on a date? Sure, I can swipe something in a few days."

Kozmo could hear the scrape of the gate as Vince opened it. She thought of the snake on the other side now, and the morning growls of the Kill Clan made her stomach turn. Vince gave them a command, and the mutants settled down.

"That won't work," the new voice insisted. "I need it now!"

"Antonio, I don't have time to get you a ride right now. The Mega Mash-up is about to start in the Dome."

"That's exactly why I . . . Nevermind. I knew you couldn't help me."

"Whoa, little brother. What's going on? What aren't you telling me?"

There was a long pause. So long Kozmo thought they might've left. But then finally, the one with the higher voice—Antonio—started talking again.

"You know how Leesa's obsessed with the Unnaturals because her Chihuahua used to be one of them? How she's always going on about how someone should help the animals when we watch the matches?"

Runt panted excitedly. "The Unnaturals! They're talking about CASTOR!"

Kozmo hushed him, her ears straining to hear through the heavy door. Vince had closed the gate and his footsteps were getting louder again.

"Tell me you're not thinking about doing anything stupid." Kozmo heard the familiar threat in Vince's voice. "Tony, that girl is screwing with your head. Look, Leesa doesn't understand how life works, okay?"

The response was sullen. "And you do? You're supposed to be some big shot gangster, but we're still scratching around underground for sky scraps."

There was a hard bump against the door of the H-Ward, and from the inside, Kozmo and Runt both flinched. The girl's strange eyes shot toward the door.

"Who do you think you're talking to?" Vince's voice was hard. "Haven't I always taken care of you? Why do you think I'm working in here, with the mayor's people?"

"I don't know!" the younger one whimpered. "I thought you hated rich sky queens like Mayor Eris."

"Oh, I do. But like I said, we just gotta play by her rules for a little while, and then everything's gonna be different for us Drain peeps. If you want to be a man, you have to make some sacrifices. You trust me?"

"Always."

"Good. Then don't screw up this gig for me by messing with the mayor's virtual reality stars."

The door shuddered again as the boy slumped against it.

"I told Leesa it was a dumb idea. I just, I wanted to make her happy, you know?"

Runt whispered that it sounded like the boy's tail was between his legs. Kozmo knew humans didn't have tails, but she knew what Runt meant.

Vince seemed to take pity on him. "Hey, Leesa likes dogs?" the trainer asked brightly. "Well, I happen to have a dog. Follow me."

Footsteps. Then the knob started to turn. They were coming inside this room!

Kozmo zoomed up to the ceiling and landed on the large rectangle of the fluorescent light. It swung wildly for a second, but when Vince and the boy walked in, they were looking down, anyway, toward Runt's cage, and didn't notice Kozmo up above.

"Wow, with that tan-and-black coloring, it looks just like the Underdog," the boy called Antonio said, peering at Runt through the bars of the cage. "Minus the wings, of course."

"Give your girl that German shepherd mutt and she'll be so smitten she'll forget all about her little jail-break scheme."

Runt whimpered in his cage, but it was the girl who let out a loud moan in protest. Antonio jerked his head around.

"Whoa. What is that?"

"*That* is Francine, the luckiest little girl in the world."

Kozmo didn't think she seemed very lucky, but she kept her mouth shut.

"She gets first crack at the serum when it's ready." He nodded toward the vials lined up along one wall. "According to those eggheads, one little drop will make everything better."

"When will it be ready?" Antonio asked. "Sky kids always get everything first. You said it was our turn!"

"Not so fast, little man. First Bruce has to figure out the right mixture. We could be testing for a long time still."

"But Vince—"

Antonio didn't get to finish his thought, though, because the chain gave way with a crash, and both humans looked up to see the light sparkling as Kozmo dangled.

"How'd that thing get in here?" Vince roared, already reaching for his pocket.

Kozmo dove down, flapping her wings and screeching as she circled the small room, but Vince already held

45

the whistle to his lips. At the first note, her body went limp, and she slammed to the floor.

Vince crouched over Kozmo and yanked on her ear, twisting it to read the tag. "K-group," he muttered. "Never heard of that one. Let's get her in the pen."

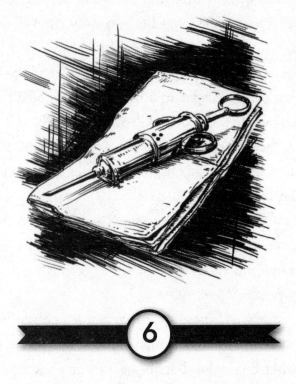

6

KOZMO WAS ON THE OTHER SIDE OF THE FENCE NOW—A place she'd never imagined she'd be. The quarantine pen had been sectioned off in the far right corner, but there was still only a flimsy wall of chicken wire separating her from the most violent mutants. They pressed against it, snouts and horns poking through the links, trying to get at her. The snake was right up front, her eyes blank, her tail rattling its warning. The kill drive overpowered everything else in her now.

Kozmo was shaking, and she could hear her breath coming quickly. She longed to run away, or to snap her wings open and soar into the rafters.

That wasn't possible anymore. Not only had she been seen, she'd been *caught*, and now a clamp rooted one of her hind legs to the floor and kept her from flying away.

On the other side of the fence, Kozmo could hear Runt barking his head off, sounding even more frenzied than he had the day before.

"Want to see an Aggression Appraisal test first?" Vince cocked an eyebrow at Antonio. "Standard protocol for new mutants."

Aggression Appraisal test.

Kozmo knew those words. When Vince wanted to thin out the Clan to make more space—and sometimes, even when he was just bored—he'd set up an Aggression Appraisal between two mutants who had been given a new trial of serum. The test never lasted long.

Soon he was dragging Runt from his cage and shoving the dog into the pen with Kozmo.

Runt seemed playful, giddy. "We get to be together now, isn't that great?" the dog panted, licking the side of Kozmo's face.

She jerked away from him, the fur along her spine rising, on high alert.

The dog's brown eyes glistened. "What's wrong?"

He didn't have any idea.

"I thought you said I could give him to Leesa," Antonio said. He knit his eyebrows in confusion.

"Come on." Vince smacked his shoulder. "This will be way more fun. Our own private match."

"I don't want to watch this," Antonio said, and fled from the room.

"Watch what? What happens?" Runt asked. "Do you know what happens?"

Kozmo knew what was *expected to* happen. In any other mutant, the kill drive would've activated. If she didn't attack Runt soon, the humans would know she was different.

Then, wouldn't she end up like the others?

Or wouldn't they make Runt hurt her instead?

And give him the shot of serum, anyway?

Kozmo didn't want to attack the dog she had spent the night curled up next to. He seemed funny and sweet, and he'd given her a name. But maybe all animals could be like that up close. Maybe it was a mistake to get close at all, when it always ended the same way—like the snake. Like Mai. Maybe a quick finish would be better.

Kozmo spread her wings. She felt the sharpened points of her teeth.

Runt sensed the change in her. He narrowed his eyes and bared his teeth, trying to look big, but his body betrayed him—his tail was between his legs and his ears lay flat to his head. He stumbled toward the snarling Kill Clan at the fence.

"You're just like them," he whimpered.

"I'm not," she protested, but Runt's howls drowned her out.

"CASTOR! Brother, help!"

The lab door banged open, but it wasn't Runt's eagle-dog brother that came to his rescue. It was one of the Yellow Six, the man with the reflective discs over his eyes—the one who looked like a fly.

"What's going on?" the fly man asked. He had to shout over the racket. "Is that K-group?" he gasped. "What's it doing in the pen?"

"Don't worry about it," Vince muttered.

But the mutants were making an even bigger commotion than Runt was, and the man turned toward the fence and spotted Kozmo. "And hey, why is this mutant in quarantine? Is that . . ." His mouth went slack, and he pressed the glass discs up on his face, squinting hard at her.

"Is that a *fox-bat*?" a woman gasped from behind her own papery yellow mask as she entered the lab. "I thought we lost them all."

They started murmuring in hushed, excited tones about K-group and gene splicing and immunity, all while staring at Kozmo intensely, scrutinizing every part of her.

Kozmo shrank back from their gaze, even though there was nowhere to go in the pen. She had spent so much of her life in the shadows hiding from humans, and with each look, Kozmo felt a greater sense of loss.

"Does Bruce know?" they asked Vince in unison.

"Not yet. I initiated an Aggression Appraisal," Vince began, "to make sure—"

"Don't you realize how valuable K-group is, you half-wit? If one survived, this would move our research forward by years! Get it out of that pen!"

The fly man, who had never spoken to Vince, opened the gate and jerked Kozmo out of the pen by the chain around her foot while Runt looked on with wide eyes.

"We need to call Bruce," the woman said.

"Why don't we wait until there's something to tell?" the man suggested quickly. "I'm sure Bruce—and the mayor—would be more excited if there was some concrete research done first."

The next thing Kozmo knew, she was clamped into a harness, her limbs splayed open. The bright light they shone in her eyes blinded her, and all she could hear was the *click click* of the yellow-clad scientists' pens as they scribbled notes. The day she'd dreaded all of her life had finally arrived.

"We have to test whether the cells are compatible," the woman said.

Kozmo saw her reaching for a sharp metal object on the tray, and she started to screech in panic.

Then the alarm sounded. The Yellow Six looked around in confusion as emergency lights flashed red and a bell droned endlessly.

The door to the lab burst open.

"Bruce!" the fly man sputtered. "We were just coming to tell you . . ."

But Bruce didn't even notice Kozmo in the harness.

"There's been some sort of mishap in the Unnaturals stadium," he shouted. "The animals are escaping. Grab your whistles. Grab the tranquilizers. My stepson is in that ring!"

"With the Invincible?" Vince asked. "With Leesa? Where's Antonio?"

Bruce's shoes squeaked along the linoleum floor as he ran, and all of the humans bolted out of the room after him. Kozmo felt her breath filling her lungs again at last.

7

Inside the golden Dome of the Unnaturals stadium, something unbelievable was happening: the fighting had stopped. The crowd watched as a group of monsters—mutant gladiators they'd seen fight viciously in the past, and who they'd expected to see fight to the death tonight—ran together across the stadium, side by side.

There was the Fearless, a saber-toothed grizzly; the Swift, a rabbit-panther; the Enforcer, an elephant-octopus; the Mighty, a zebra-bull; and the Underdog, an

53

eagle-dog. They had all broken free from their handlers and escaped their electric collars. Weirdest of all, they seemed to be working *together*.

Marcus stood watching them from across the stadium, and he was having a hard time catching his breath. In trying to free the animals, he and his friend, Leesa, had almost been killed by the vicious scorpion-tiger. The eagle-dog, who Marcus had been visiting for weeks with his brother, had swooped in at the last second, grabbing them in its talons and soaring around the Dome with the kids in tow. He, Marcus Lund, now knew what it was like to *fly*.

"They're going to do it," Leesa said, squeezing his hand. "They're really going to get away."

But despite feeling buzzy from the flight (and maybe a little bit from the way Leesa was holding his hand right now), Marcus was starting to worry.

By saving the kids from the wrath of the Invincible, the Underdog had also passed up a clear shot at escape. Now the scorpion-tiger stood firmly between Team Scratch and the exit.

It was five against one, but numbers didn't matter when the Invincible was involved—Marcus knew that better than anyone.

As a former Moniac, Marcus had warped into more

matches than he could count, and in last season's Mega Monster Mash-up, he had seen the Invincible massacre his entire team in under five minutes. Now, as Team Scratch approached and the scorpion tail arced over the white tiger head, it looked like the Invincible was hoping to break that record.

The crowd inhaled audibly, waiting for the deadly strike, and Marcus felt sick. If the eagle-dog saving his and Leesa's lives meant that these majestic animals would die, Marcus could never forgive himself.

It looked like the end.

And it was. Just not for Team Scratch. The eagle-dog darted forward and the Invincible roared. But instead of striking his opponent, the dog and his team struck a nearby stadium light post. There was a deafening *CRACK* and the crowd gasped as the post gave way, tipping slooowly at first, and then fast, and faster, until it landed with a horrible thud.

All that was left of the scorpion-tiger was the tip of his tail, pinned beneath the pole.

Fans had been promised an end of the season Monster Mash-up like they'd never seen before. They had come hoping to be shocked and awed. Marcus bet they'd never imagined something like this.

With very large mutant animals now on the loose,

the people in the stands started to panic. They streamed down from the bleachers, elbowing one another and tripping over their own feet in their hurry to reach the exits. There was no way all of Team Scratch was going to get past them through the doors.

There was now a gaping hole in the ground where the post had been ripped out of its foundation, though. You could see right down into the tunnels of the underground neighborhood of the Drain, and the animals stood around it, looking down.

"Go!" Marcus and Leesa shouted together. They knew it was Team Scratch's only shot.

The majestic eagle-dog ran over to Marcus to lick his hand in farewell, and then he turned to join the other animals as, one by one, they jumped into the hole.

8

CASTOR *ran*. HE RAN WITH HIS NECK STRAINING FORWARD, his wings streaming behind. He ran with his tongue out, gulping air. He ran until water leaked from his eyes and slobber whipped against his jowls. He ran like his lungs could hold the universe, like his legs could leap to the moon. He ran like he could never be caught. Or like he was just about to be. He didn't dare look back to find out.

Instead, the eagle-dog kept his focus on his friends up ahead. Samken lead the charge. The heavy thunder of his elephant feet echoed around them, and the eight tentacles of his trunk crashed against the sides of the narrow walls.

Jazlyn was next, checking her superior panther speed to keep pace with the group.

Castor hung back with Enza. The saber-toothed grizzly was still limping from the injuries she had sustained in the ring, and she leaned heavily against him as they ran.

Castor's heart felt ready to burst as he looked at these three odd animals. They had had their differences, and it had taken him time to trust them, but now, they were as much his family as his pack had ever been.

Castor did not know how long he had spent imprisoned at NuFormz research facility. Days blurred into numbers. He had battled in five Unnaturals matches as the Underdog. He'd fought on a team of four mutant monsters. He'd been comforted by three kindhearted humans, and had been trained by two sadists armed with whips and whistles. He had watched one mentor die a hero, and one victor die a coward. He had eaten countless meals of gritty slop.

He'd been a loner, then a fighter, then a leader.

He'd been a friend.

But Castor could barely remember the dog he had

been before—a cocky mutt whose whole world was an alley in Lion's Head, who knew how to placate the alpha and hunt raccoons and not much else.

He'd been on such a hunt the day he was taken. Castor and his little brother had strayed away from their territory, gotten into a fight with an enemy pack, and wound up cornered on a dock, staring down men in orange suits and bug masks.

How much time had passed since that day, when the men had thrown Castor in the back of their Crusher Slusher machine? How many months since they'd given him the shot that broke his bones and froze his blood, that made him sprout wings between his shoulders and grow talons between his toes?

It does not matter, he told himself. The days fell away from him the moment he leapt to his freedom.

Freedom.

Castor could practically taste the word. He could feel it in the rhythm of his four paws padding along the ground, could hear it pulsing in his chest with each breath. He could even smell it in the musty tunnel.

He felt a pang knowing that Moss, a veteran of the Unnaturals who'd spent far more time in captivity than Castor had, couldn't experience this. The zebra-bull had insisted on staying behind with the children, but

Castor vowed to come back for his old teammate. He promised himself that once they found a safe path to the Greenplains, he would come back here, even though the thought terrified him, and lead the rest of the animals to freedom.

For now, as the days of captivity fell away from him, Castor let the fear fall, too. There was the fear that had tingled in his spine with the first sharp trill of the whistle. The fear that had lived in his gut since the moment he'd stepped into the arena and seen the bloodlust of the crowd. And most of all, the fear that had threatened to crush him whenever he'd dared to dream of escape. Castor shook all of it off like dust from his fur. He left it lying at his feet, along with the electric collar in the arena. This was where his new life began.

9

MARCUS AND LEESA HUGGED EACH OTHER—FREEING THE animals had been their dream—but they didn't have much time to bask in their excitement, since things were getting pretty dangerous in the Dome.

Around them, handlers were cracking whips, a live wire on the fallen light post danced along the ground and threw sparks, and people were stampeding. Marcus heard the thunder of steps behind him and gasped, sure he was about to be trampled.

Instead, Marcus felt himself yanked off his feet as the Mighty, the old zebra-bull, bit the collar of Marcus's shirt and tossed him onto his striped back. The bull must have stayed behind when the rest of his team escaped. He doubled back and picked up Leesa as well.

The zebra-bull bucked and pivoted to get through crowd, and as a sheltered sky kid, Marcus had little experience riding bareback. He leaned forward and grabbed the bull's coarse mane for dear life, while behind him, Leesa held tight to his waist.

They were headed toward the hole the other animals had jumped into, but there were handlers all around, about to follow Team Scratch into the tunnels of the Drain.

"Look out!" Marcus screamed, but instead of turning, the Mighty quickened his stride.

The bull head-butted Horace, the red-faced manager, and then turned to deliver a hind kick to rat-faced Slim, right in the gut. Marcus felt Leesa squeeze his waist, and there was a little fluttery thrill in his chest. After seeing the handlers whip and yell at the animals in the training pen, seeing them fall already felt like victory.

But instead of following his teammates into the hole, the Mighty let out a defiant whinny, and shot a striped leg out behind him. The kick sent a food cart sailing almost a hundred feet, where it crashed into the post and toppled over, sealing off the hole where the animals had escaped.

No one would be following Team Scratch—at least not for a while.

"Marcus, stop!"

It was his stepdad, Bruce, looking furious, and Marcus figured he was in so much trouble at this point that there was no turning back.

He squeezed the Mighty's ribs with his thighs and the zebra-bull took off at full speed, plowing through the dense crowd toward the exit. Finally, they burst through the doors and outside the Dome, and Marcus felt the wind whipping through his hair.

At the first taste of freedom, the Mighty reared up, neighing with pleasure, and Marcus and Leesa both cheered.

Their victory was short-lived, though. The Unnaturals stadium was located on an island in the middle of the river, and the water surrounding it was toxic. While most of the people piled into their aircars and zipped above the water on cables toward their Skyrise apartments, Marcus and Leesa and the huge mutant animal didn't have that option.

To the east, they could see the tall glass towers of Lion's Head sparkling in the sun. Most of the security forces were sure to be concentrated on the entrance to the city, so Marcus steered the bull toward the west side of the island, where Leesa had shown him a small bridge that lead to the Greenplains.

The ground of the island was rocky, and the ride rough. The whites of the bull's eyes were wild with strain as his nostrils flared. The midday sun beat down, and a sheen of sweat formed on the Mighty's flanks.

Marcus felt his own fair skin already starting to burn under the deadly sun and pulled his shirt up over his face, while behind him, he heard Leesa coughing as she began to choke on the smog. The kids knew they couldn't survive long in this environment, but they couldn't turn back now.

When they finally reached the bridge, a truck sat parked at the entrance, its back doors open.

"Antonio!" Leesa cried with relief, as her friend stepped out of the passenger-side door. "I knew you would come through!"

But while Leesa thought her friend was here to help them, Marcus didn't trust him for a minute.

Neither did the Mighty. The zebra-bull started to pace on the shoreline, turning circles in the sand and flaring his nostrils in frustration.

Then the driver-side door opened on the truck, and as Antonio's shady brother Vince stepped out, Marcus knew his hunch had been right.

"Leesa, listen," Antonio said quickly, holding up his hands.

There was no time for conversation, though. As Vince raised a tranquilizer gun up to his shoulder, the Mighty reared up on his hind legs, and the dart hit the animal square in the chest.

"No!" Leesa screamed.

The zebra-bull crashed back down to four legs, already stumbling, and Marcus could hear the sound of choppers overhead. Craning his neck, he saw a fleet of trucks barreling toward them from the NuFormz facility.

It's over, Marcus thought, stroking the Mighty's striped neck. The bull knelt down shakily, his breathing shallow.

Marcus heard a car door close and the crunch of boots on gravel, and suddenly, he and Leesa were surrounded by people in masks and riot gear. Gloved hands pulled them off the Mighty's back, and Vince dragged the animal toward the truck, as that traitor, Antonio, stood there just staring.

"We still did it," Marcus spat defiantly as they slapped the cuffs on his wrists. "The other Unnaturals are free. This is just the beginning!"

10

Leesa's hands were wrenched behind her back, and the zip ties were digging into her wrists. She and Marcus were flanked by two uniformed men wearing dark glasses and stern expressions. But as they floated up from the island toward the Sky Towers in the mayor's own private auto-hele, Marcus grinned at her—a wild-eyed winner's smile—and Leesa felt her heart lifting, too.

Leesa had lived underground in the Drain

neighborhood for most of her life. She was used to low light, narrow walls, and musty smells. She had been to street level here and there, of course. She had seen the dirty street with the entrance to her mom's factory, where the smog was choking and the other factories crowded so close it was almost as dark as the Drain. She had seen the brown water of the polluted river and the gritty gravel that made up its bank. But she had never seen Lion's Head like *this*.

As they drifted closer, the city looked like some well-ordered forest, the buildings like sleek dark trunks reaching skyward. Their sides lit up with a million bright colors, a zillion tiny images. The auto-hele landed on the roof of the tallest of all the tall towers, and Leesa could see the tops of the other smaller, lesser towers in Lion's Head, and the cables of the aircars zigzagging between them.

And the sun! Instead of being blotted out by buildings, it was right there staring at her, and it was so bright, so beautiful, that she could hardly look at it. It was too bad this was probably going to be the last time she saw it—they were going to throw her in jail for the rest of her life.

The men marched Leesa and Marcus into the mayor's

office, and everything looked clean, and expensive, and new. Leesa didn't have to crouch beneath the ceilings, or squeeze between the furniture.

Mayor Eris sat on a plush sofa in front of a giant glass wall overlooking the city. The mayor was as pale as the white furniture that adorned her office, despite her proximity to the sun. She had dark red hair and dark red lips to match, and she moved like she had spent her whole life floating.

Despite the big space, it was starting to feel crowded as the mayor's posse of thugs filed in, along with Marcus's jerk of a stepdad, who actually *worked* for the place that tortured the animals. Everyone seemed to have backup. Leesa was the only one on her own.

"Where is your mother?" the mayor asked.

"My mom?" Leesa repeated, her voice rising nervously. "She's, um, working." Her mom was always working.

"See if you can locate Mrs. Khan," the mayor told one of her men.

"You don't have to tell her yet," Leesa said quickly. She had never been in trouble before, and the thought of her mom's disappointment was almost worse than the thought of being locked away forever.

"I think she'll want to know about owing millions of

dollars sooner rather than later, don't you?" Eris asked, raising one red eyebrow.

Leesa felt the blood drain from her face. "What?"

"You kids caused a lot of damage today. My Dome was destroyed, my star mutants lost, not to mention all the extra work my staff had to put in. Who did you think was going to pay for all of it? I'll have to add it to your family's debt."

Leesa felt sick. That debt was the whole reason she was in this mess. Her father owed the mayor for their Sky apartment, and when he couldn't pay, he started to gamble, and Leesa's Chihuahua had been turned into an Unnatural to fight. Because of the mayor, Leesa had lost her home, her dad, and her dog, and her mom was *still* trying to pay off the debt so they could move out of the Drain. Now, because of Leesa, that was never going to happen.

"Eva, they're just kids," Bruce said, leaning forward. "They didn't know what they were doing. They didn't know any—"

"We knew exactly what we were doing!" Marcus shouted, his cheeks flushing.

Mayor Eris pursed her lips. "Just tell me *why* you did it. Was it something someone told you? Was it your father?" She eyed Bruce, and Leesa saw Marcus's face twitch.

"My father's dead," Marcus answered flatly.

The mayor was undeterred. "Or your brother, the veterinarian?" she persisted. "What's his . . ." She turned to one of the cops, who whispered something. "Pete. Was it something Pete told you?"

"Pete? No."

Leesa knew the whole reason Marcus had changed his mind about the animals was because Pete told him they were real, live mutants, and not some kind of robot.

"We just did it because the animals deserved to be free," Leesa explained.

"Do you even know what happens?" Marcus asked the mayor. "How they run them until they collapse in the gym? How they whip them until they have no spirit? Have you been to where they keep them in those dirty cells?" Marcus was shouting in the mayor's face.

"Shhh," Leesa hissed. She agreed with what Marcus was saying, but she wished he wasn't saying it quite so loudly. He was only going to make things worse.

Bruce held him by the shoulders, rooting him down in the chair. "Marcus, you don't know how important the mutants are, what they could mean for—"

Mayor Eris shot Bruce a look. "They're important," she said carefully, "for morale. We've had some hard times in Lion's Head. The people need something to look

70

forward to. Something to root for."

Bruce sighed. "Look, Eva, are we done here? I have to get the boy home to his mother."

Leesa noticed how Bruce called Marcus "the boy," like he could be any boy, anyone's son. Leesa hadn't seen Baba in months, and he certainly hadn't always been the father she'd wished for, but at least he wasn't Bruce.

Mayor Eris pressed her red lips together. "Go. We can sort out *your* debt later."

"And Peter?"

"A few of our stars need medical attention."

Leesa watched Marcus stand. She stared at him as he grabbed his bag. She could not believe he was just going to leave her here. When he met her eyes, he looked sheepish.

"Maybe we could, um, take Leesa home with us?" Marcus said. For all his macho talk about standing up to Bruce, his voice sure did sound small.

"We can't release her until her legal guardian comes," Mayor Eris said.

With a nod from the mayor, the goons shuffled out behind Marcus and Bruce, and Leesa suddenly felt very small and very vulnerable. Trying to avoid Mayor Eris's piercing look, Leesa looked down at the dumb decorative pillows, across the room at the pointless fake flowers, and finally out the window.

She could see inside some of the Sky apartments, and thinking about how hard her mom worked and how they would never get out of the Drain now, Leesa felt her eyes welling with tears.

"Impressive view, hmm?" The mayor's tone was mild, but Leesa bristled. Was she making fun of her?

"I thought there would be clouds," Leesa answered. Antonio and everyone she knew in the Drain had said that the rich were so stupid because all they ever saw was clouds, and their brains became airy balls of fluff. But from where she sat, looking out of the windowed walls of the mayor's office, Leesa saw clear blue.

"Not for a while now." The mayor walked close to the glass and hugged her arms around her willowy body. "The sun is too hot. It burns away all the moisture."

"It's pretty, though."

Leesa hadn't meant to say that aloud, but the mayor nodded vigorously. "Maybe one day we'll all be able to go out there and feel it on our skin."

And maybe one day I'll live in this penthouse, Leesa thought.

"My daughter used to love the sun," the mayor said absently.

Leesa was curious, despite herself. For years, Leesa could remember watching the mayor speak. Her husband, a droopy little man, always stood behind her like an afterthought, but Leesa couldn't remember ever seeing any kids. And why had she said "used to"?

"You have a daughter?"

"Mmmhmm." The mayor drifted over and took the seat Marcus had left, next to Leesa. She clicked a button, and a hologram materialized in front of them.

A waifish girl was strapped into a hoverchair, but she was laughing. A small lizard perched on her head, and a white tiger was licking her face.

"She's just about your age," Mayor Eris said. "Maybe you could meet sometime. I know she's lonely, and I bet you two would get along, especially since you both love animals—"

"Does she love watching them suffer, like you?" Leesa spat before she could help herself.

The mayor's face tightened. "Look, I'm willing to look past the damages," Eva Eris said. "But I want us to understand each other, Leesa."

"Okay. . . ." Leesa felt uneasy.

"Your friend Marcus means well, I can see that. But he sees things as good and bad. You're smarter than that, aren't you? Those of us who have lived through tough things, we know that life is a little more complicated, don't we?"

Leesa thought of her father's gambling—how he believed he could get Pookie back for her, even though it had cost him the house and then his marriage. She thought of Antonio—how he could be so sweet to her, but he was so desperate to impress his brother that it made him turn into a jerk. She thought of Marcus—how he saw one real Unnaturals match and just instantly flipped from an ultra-fanboy Moniac into an animal-rights activist, literally overnight. How he couldn't understand how she'd needed to see so many matches over the years—every single match Pookie was in—even though she thought the whole business was wrong.

Leesa thought of how she didn't regret freeing the Unnaturals for a second, but how she had her mom to think about, too.

Complicated was an understatement.

Mayor Eris pet Leesa's arm, her nails brushing against Leesa's skin like some sort of insect, and Leesa flinched.

"What I'm saying is that sometimes we need to do things that other people might see as questionable, but that we know in our hearts are for good. And everything I do, I do for Francine."

The mayor sat back, her face pinched, and Leesa thought how much she would've loved this big, clean room, if the mayor hadn't made it feel so dirty.

11

IN THE UNDERGROUND ROOM, THE ALARMS WERE WAILING. The mutants hurled themselves against the fences in a frenzy, and next to them in the pen, the dog was still cowering low with its tail between its legs. That was Kozmo's fault.

She felt that strange urge to comfort Runt again, to tell him that it would be all right, but Kozmo knew better. She was strapped to a harness with her wings splayed, Runt was locked in a cage, and the humans would be back eventually. It was only going to get worse from here.

Suddenly, there was a crash from across the room. Kozmo struggled to see what was happening, but the clamp around her neck restricted her movements.

"What is it?" she called out to Runt, but the dog's attention was focused away from her.

The H-Ward door was wide open, and a giant lizard slithered into view. It must've snuck in there during the commotion.

It crept past all the cages with the animals snarling and hissing and stopped in front of Runt's pen. Instead of paws like Kozmo, the lizard had long, green digits. It began to work at the latch on the pen, and there was a soft click. So that was how it must've gotten out of the cage.

Kozmo could smell the fear coming off Runt's fur in waves as he waited for the lizard to charge.

Instead she just pulled the door to the pen open and she scurried over to Kozmo. The lizard picked at the clamp around her neck with her nails.

Runt barked a sharp warning. "Don't! She's dangerous! Bad like the others! She almost attacked me!"

"I think she's trying to help," Kozmo answered, but then Runt flashed his teeth, and she realized he was talking about her.

The lizard didn't listen, though, and soon she had the clamp open. The moment Kozmo could open her wings, she shot up into the rafters, away from all the other animals. It was only when she was safe in her nest that she thought to check on Runt.

The dog trotted out of the pen with a floppy-tongued grin, and he let out a little yip of surprise when the lizard grabbed him with its powerful tail, dragging him past the vicious mutants snarling from behind the fences, and toward EXIT.

"Hey!" Runt barked, his eyes bugging out in fear. "Let me go!"

Kozmo zoomed down after them, but she was too late. She saw the green flicker of the lizard's tail as it disappeared with Runt into the world of humans, and then she slammed into the locked door, crumpling into a heap on the linoleum.

"Wait," Kozmo squeaked. "Wait . . ."

12

WHEN THEY LEFT THE MAYOR'S OFFICE, MARCUS THOUGHT he was in for a lecture, but Bruce didn't say anything. He held the back of Marcus's neck, not hard, but firmly enough that Marcus hunched forward, his long hair falling into his eyes as his stepfather steered him toward the aircar. Bruce had to punch in the coordinates twice, irritation making his fingers clumsy.

"I didn't—" Marcus started, but Bruce held up a hand, cutting off any discussion.

Fine. Marcus slumped down in the seat and stared out the window. As the aircar zipped along the cables across Lion's Head, the view soon erased any concern about lame old Bruce. The Sky Towers were packed close together, so from his own room, all Marcus could see was the dark glass sides of other buildings. But from all the way up here, even in the dusk, he could see clear across the river to the hazy mass of trees on the other side.

The Greenplains.

Had the Underdog and the other mutants made it there yet? Marcus hoped so. The thought made him giddy, and he knew that no matter what the mayor said, or how long he was grounded for, helping the animals escape was totally worth it. He had done what everyone else was too chicken to do—pretty rad, if he did say so himself.

Marcus grinned, but then he felt his stomach drop. Usually Bruce was a real stiff, obsessed with rules and cautious in the extreme. But today, not only had he switched off the aircar's auto settings, but he seemed to have unclamped the cable break, too. The car was gaining speed as it sloped down, dropping stories by the second.

Marcus liked a little risk—he had enough skateboarding scars to prove it—but he could see the cable throwing off sparks from the friction, and the way Bruce was staring straight ahead with his jaw all clenched up was really starting to freak Marcus out.

They fell faster, and faster still, and though Marcus would not let himself cry out to Bruce, he had to bite hard on the inside of his cheek to keep from screaming. Just when it seemed like the car might snap right off its track and send them tumbling to their deaths, Bruce hit a switch and they jerked to a sudden stop at the 247th floor of their Skyrise.

"Home safe and sound," Bruce said in a flat voice verging on disappointed. He stepped out of the aircar unceremoniously, and Marcus stared after him with bug eyes, waiting for his heart rate to slow back to normal.

When they walked into the apartment, it was a sharp contrast to the silence of the trip. Marcus's mom screamed his name, yanked him into a stifling hug, and then launched into five minutes of constant, weepy scolding.

She cared about rules, too, but for different reasons than Bruce did. It was mainly because, since his real dad had passed away a while back, Marcus's mom had become convinced that any time he or his brother left the apartment and ventured out of her sight, they were at imminent risk of death, too. It had taken Marcus *years* to convince her to let him skate, and even then she made him wear a bubble suit and totally lost it when he'd sprained his wrist attempting a kick flip a few weeks back.

Hearing that her youngest son had not only been *below the 100th story skyline*, but had been *in the proximity of deadly monsters* and *exposed to unfiltered air* and *the full force of the sun*? Well, that sent her completely over the edge.

"What were you thinking? What if something had happened to you? You could've gotten hurt! Or worse!" She checked his face for bruises, his body for broken bones. She kept tilting his head back and looking up his nose, like his brains were about to start gushing out or something. "You're grounded, young man. Do you hear me? Until you're eighteen. Until you're thirty!"

That was pretty much what Marcus had expected. Still worth it.

He went to his room to turn on his simulink, anxious to see what the media was saying about the big escape. Flipping through the headlines, Marcus saw that people were mostly complaining about the issues that the reconstruction of the Dome was going to cause, since the next Unnaturals season would likely be delayed. There were think pieces on the new void in virtual distraction, videos of kids complaining about their season tickets, and hysterical articles about match-withdrawal-induced depression in tweens.

Only one person was looking at the mayor and Mega Media critically or talking about the animals at all, and that was Joni Juniper.

Joni was the former Matchmaker—the announcer and commentator at every Unnaturals match. Marcus had known her face well from warping into matches, but now Joni was actually dating his brother, Pete, and Marcus suspected she was the one who'd talked him into standing up for the animals.

His brother had caught Marcus and Leesa breaking into the Dome, and rather than turn them away or even turn them in, Pete had actually *helped* them, which cost him his job as the monster medic, at the very least. It took guts. Joni was notably absent from the Matchmaker's booth, her own small form of protest. Yet here she was, digging up dirt!

It was just a self-posted channel, but Joni was acting like a real reporter, and it looked like she already had a lot of followers—most of them probably Moniacs, but still. And while every other commentator had been talking about how this affected their own lives and what this meant for the future of entertainment, Joni was actually talking about the corruption.

"Many here in Lion's Head are shocked at the notable veil of secrecy surrounding these events. Access to NuFormz island has been cut off, and while Mega Media had assured the public that the mutants were in a highly controlled environment and citizens were not at risk, we have recently obtained information to suggest that the animals were being injected with a serum designed to make them ultraviolent for matches."

Marcus sat up straight. It was good that people thought the mutants were dangerous—it would give them a better chance at escaping if no one went near them—but was the thing about the serum true? He'd have to ask Pete.

Where was his brother, anyway?

"Is Pete still helping the injured animals?" he asked, walking back into the living room.

"I thought he was coming back with you?" His mom and Bruce locked eyes over Marcus's head, her forehead creasing. "Bruce?" she said sharply.

"I don't know." Bruce sighed.

Marcus looked up, feeling worried for the first

time—Bruce almost never admitted that he didn't know something.

His stepdad was already headed back toward the door. "I'll go find out what she wants," Marcus heard him mutter.

13

The squeaks announce a visitor. You guzzle milk from the nozzle. You snuggle your littermates. The prayer of "you're special, special, special," whispered over and over.

It's always the same, until the day everything changes.

This time, you aren't taken back to the nest.

Instead, you are placed inside a small

container with sides too smooth to scale. There is a whirring overhead that makes the icy air rush over your fur, which is not much more than fuzz, and you shiver. You pull your tail up to your chest to keep warm, since the others are no longer beside you.

You can still hear them, though. The pitch of their screeches tells you that they are enduring the same things you are: more gloved hands poking and prodding and pulling.

The other unfamiliar sounds blend together—the chatter of people as they communicate, the squeak on the floor that tells you the man is coming, the click click and scritch scritch after each test—so you focus on the screeching of your littermates, and find comfort.

The screeching gradually gets less frequent, though, and at last, yours is the only voice you hear. You stop yelling, too, because there is no one to hear you, and the next time a gloved hand picks you up, you freeze, because you are so scared to be alone in the world.

"Looks like we lost this one, too."

The man comes over, his shoes going squeak squeak squeak, and now that there is no more screeching to focus on, he is hard to ignore. He pokes you, and you think your heart will stop in your chest.

"That's the last of Vulpes pongo chiroptera then. I really thought we had it—the perfect combination."

"Do you want me to dissect it?" the human holding you in her hands asks.

The man does not answer for a long time, so you play the woman's sounds in your head over and over, wondering what they mean.

Click click, scritch scritch.

"Bruce?"

Click click.

"Sorry, just jotting down some notes," the man says. "Don't bother with the autopsies this time. It doesn't matter, anyway. We're right back where we started."

14

KOZMO WOKE TO THE SOUND OF BRUCE'S VOICE, AND SHE froze. Below her, the door to H-Ward still hung open, but now she could see the shadows of people moving inside.

"This can't be happening," Bruce moaned. "This could mean we're right back where we started. My work . . ."

"Your *work*?" a woman's voice trembled. It was high pitched and full of rage—tonally, it reminded Kozmo of the kill drive being activated. "You're telling me she just vanished, too? Is there no area in this whole place that is secure?"

Kozmo's ears perked up. Were they talking about her? One of the Yellow Six must've told him they'd found her.

"What kind of lab are you running, Bruce? Are there no protocols?"

"Vince deals with security. I just—"

"You just stormed in here screaming about an emergency and telling everyone to abandon their posts," Vince said, entering the lab.

Bruce stormed out of H-Ward, but he stopped short when he saw that Vince led two mutants behind him on gold chains. One was a tiger with a scorpion's stinging tail, and the other was a squat Komodo dragon with a rhinoceros's horned head—Kozmo had never seen either before, but after so long in the room, she quickly recognized different animal parts.

"Doctor Petey fixed these guys up good as new with a little of your magic sauce," Vince said. "The zebra-bull is still out cold, but he should come around. No sign of the others yet."

The woman Bruce had been talking to followed him out of H-Ward, and the air seemed to shift around her. For a moment, Kozmo thought she was a mutant instead of a human, since she wore a white furry covering puffed around her shoulders. Her hair was the color of blood, and her skin looked like the blood had been sucked right out of it.

"Those violent creatures are still on the loose? What if they find her before we do?"

"Not a chance," Vince said, and Kozmo noticed that he seemed to be puffing himself up, too. Only Bruce was shrinking back behind them. "I've been working with my Clan here, and they've been evolving without ol' Bruce's help. Got 'em so trained they'll do anything I command."

The red-plumed woman seemed uncertain. "They can track?"

"All I've gotta do is tell them to play a little game of fetch, and they'll retrieve the prize, and kill anything else that gets in the way."

"Only if you take Laringo," she said, scratching the white tiger behind the ears. "He'll keep the others in line."

"Eva, you can't be serious," Bruce scoffed. "You're going to trust this gangster and a snarling group of failed test subjects to find her?"

"*Your* failed test subjects," the red-plumed woman said sharply. "Right now, I trust just about anyone more than I trust you, Bruce. After what you did . . ."

"What I did was research!" Pink dots appeared on Bruce's cheekbones.

"I need results, not research. You've had more than enough chances to get the serum right, all the test subjects and funding you could want. Thanks to that stunt your kids pulled and that twit Joni Juniper, we've got lots of eyes on us now, so I can't have any more animals coming in. We're moving on to the next phase."

"I already have volunteers," Vince said.

Bruce looked at him with disgust, and then turned back to the woman. "Eva, I can't support that. It's unethical. You can't put one life at risk to save another."

"No? Don't forget I have your stepson."

"You can't just hold Pete indefinitely for no reason!"

The woman smiled with lips as red as her hair, and to Kozmo, it looked like a gash against the white of her skin. "I'm sure the media will give us a reason. Give them a little whiff of meat and they'll dig up a carcass."

Bruce took a deep breath in and out. "I'm on the verge of a breakthrough. I can find it . . ."

"Two weeks," the woman said. "And in the meantime, I want her found, whatever it takes."

In her nest, Kozmo shuddered. Vince and his Kill Clan were hunting her now, and when they found her, she would be back in that harness. Back under Bruce's microscope. And soon he would silence her screeches, too.

If only she had left with Runt and the lizard! If only there were another way out!

Kozmo rocked herself back and forth rhythmically, trying to brainstorm what to do. It was hard to concentrate, though, because each time she clenched her toes on the metal slats, the screw in the vent got a little looser, thanks to the snake from earlier. Before long, the vent would come completely free, and she wouldn't even be able to hang from it to relax.

Kozmo looked up toward her toes suddenly. What if the snake had been right? What if Kozmo had made her home on a secret door all along?

While the humans argued below, Kozmo worked ever so slowly and ever so quietly to unscrew the vent. When it finally came free, she poked her head up through the hole just to see if *outside* was as real as the snake had claimed.

Her head was out of the room, and what she saw was very different from what she was used to. There was a tunnel that seemed to go on forever. The air smelled earthy. Kozmo could go farther, she realized. Nothing was holding her inside the room—not the men, not a cage. Was this the freedom the snake had been dreaming of?

Kozmo hesitated. She did not know where the path led. She knew the room, knew every inch of its walls. She understood its secrets, and she had learned how to survive. But that was over now that the humans knew she was different.

The lizard was different, too, it seemed. It had not attacked, and it had not been dazed. It had actually helped another animal, which was something the creature had never witnessed.

There was no one like her left in the room. No littermates. No Runt. No lizard. Only Bruce and his serums.

Kozmo climbed up into the tunnel, leaving the room and all of its dangers behind. Sound traveled well in the tunnel, and it wasn't long before Kozmo's triangular ears twitched.

"Hello?" she called. Perhaps she'd already found the dog and the lizard?

But the echo back told her it was a pack of animals, not just two, and they were stampeding. They were almost upon her! Kozmo fled up to the ceiling in a panic and wedged herself into a tight crevice.

The first mutant she saw was a giant gray beast with eight writhing tentacles. Its body took up the whole tunnel. It barreled toward her, making the walls quake. She huddled tighter in the crack, only poking her head out when they had passed. The last thing she could see was the backside of something four legged and furry down the tunnel, with ragged wings trailing behind it.

It was a group of mutants—out of their cages! Were these the violent creatures the red-haired woman had said would tear her apart? If their kill drive was unregulated, they would attack anything that came in their path.

Including the dog and the lizard!

Kozmo raised her voice through the tunnels, hoping to warn them.

"Friends!" she called, remembering the word Runt had used, but her screeches bounced back to her, unanswered.

15

"Where are we going?" Enza asked, her voice echoing into the void. She must've asked that question ten times already.

"The Greenplains," Jazlyn answered once more. Castor gave her a grateful smile. His friend was ever patient, ever positive.

Still, Castor knew she had to be getting tired. They all were. The initial rush of excitement had long since faded, and with it, the feeling that they were untouchable.

It was replaced by a dull anxiety that Castor could sense humming in the spaces between them, and a profound exhaustion that none of them could give into—not yet.

He'd imagined escape as something quick, something final. But once you escaped, you had to *keep* escaping, or else you'd be caught again.

"Just a little farther," Castor said. It sounded unconvincing, even to him.

"You said that two hours ago," Enza huffed. With each limping step, the grizzly leaned more of her weight onto Castor's shoulder. Her long, striped tail hung limply behind her, dragging through the grime. "I thought you were supposed to lead us out of here."

Castor grit his teeth in response. He might've been raised on the streets of Lion's Head, but he'd sure never been inside the tunnels that ran beneath them before. He thought he knew where the Greenplains was located— back in the arena, when the red door had swung open, he had glimpsed the trees just across the river. But then the handlers had rushed in, and Laringo had attacked, and Team Scratch jumped into the hole in the floor on a wing and a prayer and . . .

And now Castor had no idea where they were.

A little farther. One step, then another. Forward was what mattered.

Sometimes it was hard to tell that they were moving at all, though. It didn't help that everywhere they went, the path looked the same: dim light and a damp floor, with iron support beams curving up the rounded walls every few feet. It might've been the adrenaline crashing out of his system, but that endless, repetitive spiral started to make Castor dizzy. It started to mess with his mind.

The rounded beams looked like ribs, and Castor felt sure they were in the belly of some giant beast. As Samken and Jazlyn walked ahead, their long shadows seemed to take on new shapes, reaching for Castor's ankles, dragging him down. And somewhere, maybe locked away in some forgotten corner of his mind, Castor could swear he heard Runt's voice calling his name.

"What was that?" Samken said, his eyes round. The octo-elephant paused with one tree-like leg still lifted in the air, the skin of his enormous gray ears rippling. "Did you hear that?"

Castor snapped out of his daze, his ears standing tall and alert. Had Runt's voice been more than a hallucination?

But the faint sound Castor heard was definitely not his brother. It was some kind of . . . screeching. He froze, and the hackles on his back stood straight up.

For several minutes there was nothing, so finally the group started to move again, cautiously, but quickly, too.

Then, *"EEEEEEE!"* It was louder this time, and the echo of the tunnel made it seem like the sound was coming from all around them.

"Ah!" Samken gasped. He recoiled backward, and Jazlyn, Castor, and Enza tripped over one another, crashing into his broad backside.

"It's okay, Sammy," Jazlyn said soothingly, rubbing her sleek panther coat against him. "It's probably just mice."

"M-m-mice?" Samken sputtered. He shot a wild look at the ground beneath him. "But I'm scared of mice!"

"Rats, more likely," Enza said, flashing her saber teeth. When she was grouchy, it seemed she couldn't stop herself from tormenting everyone else.

"RATS? We need to get out of here!" Samken wailed. He could be fiercely intimidating in the arena, but Castor knew that half of that had been performance art. When it came to real-world obstacles, Samken's terror was even bigger than he was.

Castor shot Enza an exasperated look, and her feline eyes dilated with satisfaction.

Samken took shaky, tentative steps forward, his head on a constant swivel as he searched for another path, and Jazlyn loped along by his side, murmuring soothing words. "If we do see a mouse, remember, we've got a half tiger on our side, and Enza's a great hunter. You've seen her pounce in the arena!"

Jazlyn was half panther herself now, and Castor was about to protest that he wasn't a bad rat hunter, either. But when he saw the way the saber-toothed grizzly was puffing out her chest and walking a little taller, leaning on him a little less, Castor kept his mouth shut. Somehow, Jazlyn always seemed to know what each of them needed.

"How about that way?" Samken pointed one of his trunks to the right at the next split. "You don't think rats could be down there, too, do you?"

Castor had seen enough rats in the alleys of Lion's Head to know that there had to be millions of them underground whichever way they turned, but Samken didn't need to know that. The truth was, Castor didn't think it was the rats that were making those sounds. Rats *scritch scritch*ed, and *squeak squeak*ed, but these screeches sounded like something else. Something bigger.

"Looks good to me," Castor answered. They were lost, anyway. If turning down a new path helped them avoid whatever creature lay hidden in the darkness, Castor was all for it.

As it turned out, this path was a little bit different. There were the same rib-like beams and the same hard, damp ground, but now there was also a set of raised metal rails running down the center. Castor had no idea what to make of them.

"They're probably from the old trains!" Jazlyn said excitedly, her white ears flopping forward.

"Trains?" Castor repeated. He'd never heard of such a thing. He put his nose to one track, sniffing the metal cautiously. It smelled like old grease and rust.

Luckily, Jazlyn had a lot more experience with human things than the rest of them. She'd lived as a pet, and in a science classroom, and in a research lab, all before coming to NuFormz, and she had learned a whole lot just from paying attention. "It's how the humans got around before the aircars. There used to be a whole subway system down here," she explained. "One of these lines definitely would've led across the river to the Green-plains!"

At the mention of the Greenplains, the animals perked up. Castor's tail began to wag as he broke into a trot. Even Samken grew more confident. He pulled his shoulders back, and his big feet were moving so quickly that Castor could feel the vibrations around them, sending little showers of dirt trickling from the ceiling.

When they rounded the next bend, the sudden flood of light made Castor press his front legs into the ground, skidding. In the fraction of a second before his hind quarters came to a stop, Castor registered three things: a large metal box that cut off the track in front of them; a wide platform checkered with tents and small leaning buildings made from materials from the trash mountains; and the small group of humans that stood in front of them with their mouths slack—drawn out, no doubt, by the shaking of the tunnel.

One of the humans was a dark-haired boy with a lanky build, and Castor recognized him from a day, months ago, at the Pit where the mutants trained. It was the boy who had been with Leesa—Pookie's Leesa—and Castor remembered how the boy had talked to her like he was growling, and how this boy had looked at the good boy Marcus like he had stolen his bone, and Castor remembered how in that moment, all the way across the gym, he'd thought about biting this boy's leg.

Now, as the boy turned his head to shout to someone, Castor's body caught up with his mind, and he barked to his teammates, "RUN!"

Jazlyn had already pivoted and was racing back toward them. The look on her face reminded them all what capture would look like, and somehow they found new reserves of energy. Enza did not need Castor's help at all as they tore through the tunnel, and if the walls were shaking before, now the rhythm of Samken's feet was so thunderous it sounded like the earth would cave in around them. They did not think about the path. They just thought *GO, GO, GO.*

Until the mouth of the tunnel narrowed suddenly.

"Why are we stopping?" Enza snapped. "Come on, Samken, move it!"

"I . . . I can't," the octo-elephant said in a small voice. "I think I'm stuck."

16

Samken wasn't the only one who was stuck. Jazlyn was in front of the mutant elephant, and Castor and Enza were trapped behind, and the walls squeezed around Samken's middle, preventing any of them from getting through.

"Stay calm," Castor said, though inside, he was panicking. "Samken, try to hold your breath in. Enza, help me push."

Jazlyn peered at them through Samken's legs. "I'll

pull from the front, too," she said. "Sammy, hold on to me tight with your trunks."

Bracing their shoulders against Samken's backside, Castor and Enza heaved and huffed, and Jazlyn pulled and tugged, but no matter how hard they tried, Samken was wedged tight.

"I'm sorry." They heard Samken's muffled voice say from the other side. "This is all my fault." They could feel the tremors as he began to weep.

Eventually, Castor was panting so hard they had to stop. He slid down onto the floor, feeling the damp dirt cold on his belly. He laid his head on his paws. *How long until the humans find them?* he wondered. *How long until they are back behind bars?*

Enza stood over him, her great bear head cocked in disbelief. "What are *you* doing?" she demanded.

Castor just stared at the ground. Wasn't it obvious? *Giving up.*

"Unbelievable," Enza said in disgust. "I almost died once, remember?"

How could Castor forget? Enza had been following his advice, trying to be brave, but she was no match for Laringo's scorpion stinger and slashing claws in the arena. It had been a devastating blow to the team.

"And you had the nerve to come visit me," she

continued. "To tell me that I'd get better, that we would escape, that the next open door we saw, we'd jump through together."

"You did," Castor said dully. "And we did. And look where it got us."

"No," Enza snapped. "There *was* no open door. Because there's almost never just a door left wide open for you to walk through. Moss kicked down that light post and *made* a door, and *that's* the only reason we got away."

"So what?" Castor asked. "We make a door?"

"We make a door."

Enza stood up on her hind legs, rising to her full height, and pressed her paws against the rounded wall near Samken. Tilting her head, she set the sharp points of her saber teeth on the ceiling. As she began to scratch with her teeth, Castor watched the ceiling start to crumble. Samken shifted his weight, and a little more gave way.

Still, it was only a little bit. Castor couldn't imagine enough of the ceiling opening up to get all of them out of here. "Enza, are you crazy? That's going to take forever."

"Yeah, by myself. But not if we work together. Boy, freedom sure has made you lazy."

17

Instead of being punished, Leesa, a Draino criminal, was being pampered. Somehow, she had ended up staying in the fanciest Sky Tower of them all, on a bed that felt like a cloud, in a room that smelled like coconuts and chocolate. Francine's room.

When they hadn't reached her mom at the factory and it was past eight, Leesa knew that she must be asleep in the apartment. Her mom only slept a few hours a night between her jobs, but when she slept, it was a heavy sleep.

"Just go bang on the apartment door," Leesa told them, but since the mayor's men had no intention of going into the Drain, Leesa was stuck here for the night.

She figured they'd stick her in a jail cell or something, considering the trouble she was in, but instead, a plump woman cut the zip ties from Leesa's wrists, gave her a pair of pajamas, and led her to a room entirely decked out in bubblegum pink.

Not really Leesa's style, but Francine didn't seem to be around. Neither did the tiger Leesa had seen in the hologram, or the lizard—though an amphibian tank did sit empty across the room. It creeped Leesa out, but it had been a long day, and it didn't stop her from falling right to sleep.

Leesa woke, disoriented, as a voice announced through a speaker in the wall that her mother was here, and that she was to report to the mayor's office. Leesa scrambled out of bed, and pulled on her combat boots and shirt, which still had the musky smell of the Unnaturals Dome on them. She couldn't wait to get home and change.

But just as she was about to leave, Leesa spotted a bookcase overflowing with books—real, old-fashioned books—and she couldn't resist grabbing one. This sky girl had everything. She'd never miss it. Leesa shoved the book in the pocket of her black hooded sweatshirt, and went to find her mom.

When she opened the door to the office, her mom was there, but she looked nervous, and as soon as Leesa stepped in, the flashbulbs went off. The mayor had a big announcement, and she wanted Leesa to be a part of it.

"Thank you for showing me it was time for a change," Mayor Eris said to Leesa under her breath. Then she turned to the screens of reporters and told them, "This is Leesa. Our hero!"

The mayor's smile was as white and pristine as everything else in her office, but something about it was unsettling. Like the way her skin seemed a little too tight and her eyes never seemed to close fully when she blinked. To Leesa, she looked like a doll—manufactured.

"Things have gone on too long as they were," she declared, gripping Leesa around the shoulders. "It's time for a new era."

18

The City Speak clicked on and announced that a mandatory press conference would interrupt normal programming.

Marcus and his parents sat on the couch and looked out the window wall of their living room. The Sky Towers around them were still flashing all different images on each one of their glass windows—ads and warnings and news clips and reruns of old Unnaturals matches.

Then, all at once, every screen went black. When they clicked back on, they all showed the same image: Mayor Eris, streaming live from her office, where Marcus had sat less than a day ago.

"What happened yesterday at the Unnaturals Dome was a tragedy," the mayor's one thousand mouths said together.

Mayor Eris's voice came out of speakers in their wall, so it sounded like she was right there with them. Her tone was a lot different yesterday. More people must have seen Joni's broadcast than he'd thought.

"During a security oversight, four mutant animals managed to evade their handlers. In the ensuing chaos, we regret that people were injured. Two women were trampled by other members of the audience, resulting in a punctured lung and a sprained arm. One man suffered a heart attack. And several staff members who were trying to get control of the animals were attacked while doing their jobs. Unfortunately, the mutants were able to escape and are still at large."

Marcus wanted to cheer and pump his fists in the air, but his mom and Bruce were somber, putting a real damper on the situation. He wondered how other people were reacting behind all those Sky Tower windows. He knew at least one person in Lion's Head would be happy, and he wished he could be celebrating with Leesa right now instead of trapped in this stifling room with his parents.

Right then, Leesa's face flashed on the screen.

"Thankfully, with inside knowledge of a corrupt employee, this young lady took action and risked her own life to prevent a real tragedy. For that act of valor, Lion's Head owes her a great debt."

Why is Leesa getting all the credit? Marcus thought sourly. *They had planned this together from the beginning.*

"Still," continued Mayor Eris, "this was a devastating turn of events for Mega Media, a company that has always strived to provide the best entertainment value," Mayor Eris continued. "As part-owner of the company, I am confident in Mega Media's safety standards and protocol. However, as mayor of Lion's

Head, it has been my stated mission from the start to protect its citizens. In my three terms served, we have tripled the thickness of UV glass on new towers, eliminated produce and with it many food-borne diseases, and reduced sky crime by nearly 80 percent."

The mayor paused here to stare out meaningfully at all the people watching from their homes.

"I want to remind citizens that the escaped animals are very dangerous and should be treated with extreme caution. We are already developing technology to quickly apprehend them, but Mega Media takes responsibility for creating something that is a demonstrated risk to the citizens of Lion's Head. After careful consideration, we have decided that this will be the Unnaturals' final season."

Marcus actually gasped. "Did she just say what I think she said?" This was beyond what he had dared to hope for.

No one else had expected it, either. His mom's mouth hung open, and Bruce was leaning far forward, clasping his hands between his knees. Watching his stepdad hanging on the mayor's words—words *he* had inspired—Marcus couldn't help smirking a little.

They were *canceling* the Unnaturals? *Completely?*

"NuFormz will discontinue its mutant gladiator program to focus on research that can more directly benefit the needs of the community long-term. Thank you."

The screens went black again, but as soon as they came back on, the feeds were already full of commentators volleying questions and Moniac fans threatening to riot. It was clear that not everyone was happy with this decision.

Marcus, however, was elated. "I guess this means you're out of the job then, huh, Bruce?" he asked.

"Marcus." His mom gave him a look that said he should stop talking if he knew what was good for him.

Bruce pinched the bridge of his nose and rubbed his eyes. He didn't say anything for a long time, and Marcus actually felt a little guilty. Only for a second, though, because when Bruce did speak, he was the same condescending jerk as always.

"I wish the world really was as simple as you think it is, Marcus. First the Unnaturals reality show is your favorite thing in the world, then it's the worst thing that ever happened in Lion's Head. First the mayor is your number one enemy, and now I am. . . ."

"No," Marcus answered coolly. "You've always been at the top of my list, Bruce."

Bruce blinked at him. "You really think I orchestrated this whole thing, don't you?" He shook his head in disbelief, but Marcus didn't budge. "Let me ask you something, kiddo. Who do you think has been profiting from the matches all these years? Because I'm certainly not rich. And what do you think is going to happen to those animals now—the ones you *saved*? Who do you think is going to have to clean up your little mess?"

Marcus tuned out Bruce's words. All that mattered was that the mess was over . . . right?

19

After the mayor's big announcement, Leesa felt like her insides were all tangled up. She was relieved, of course. This was what she'd wanted for years, what she'd tried so hard to make happen. The Unnaturals games were finally over, and now no more animals would have to go through what her beloved pet Chihuahua-turned-mutant-spider had.

But the way the mayor had spun the story made Leesa feel queasy. She had acted like the animals were evil or something. Like Leesa knew things she didn't. Like Marcus hadn't been part of it at all.

It was still a huge win; even her mom said so. Oh, Leesa's mom had been plenty angry with her—she wasn't cool with anything that could jeopardize Leesa's future chances of success, and doing something that put lots of people in danger and caused major damage to property definitely fell in that category—but that didn't mean she wasn't still proud of her daughter.

One of the mayor's goons had escorted them all the way home from the mayor's office, which took forever and was super embarrassing. Even after they took the elevator down almost eight hundred flights, they were far from home. The mayor's Skyrise was right on the river on the west side of Lion's Head, and while the Drain sprawled under the entire city, under the river, and all the way to the Greenplains, the only entrance to the underground neighborhood was on the southeastern tip, right on the border of the trash mountains.

Leesa and her mom traveled across Lion's Head using the covered footbridges connecting all the buildings. The whole time, the security guy was right behind them with his baton, acting like they were the scary animals, about to attack, but Leesa's mom held up her head the whole time. They had to go outside to access one of the stairwells that would take them down into the tunnels, and they could see the press conference already airing reruns for anyone who had missed it.

Even though they'd been at the live feed, they stopped to watch, anyway, and Leesa's mom put her arm around Leesa's shoulders. They stood on the top step of the Drain, so small next to the buildings, and faced the infinite faces of the mayor. Her eyes reflected like that, over and over across multiple buildings, made it seem like she was watching them from everywhere, but at least they couldn't hear her voice—everyone else was listening to the sound inside their homes. The lies were silent this time. Eris's words couldn't touch them.

When they got to the underground, everyone was talking about it, of course. Unlike the sky city, where people stayed locked up inside by themselves, the underground neighborhood was buzzing with chatter and life.

No one seemed happy. They didn't care about the entertainment—only sky people could actually afford fancy things like warp screens for a virtual reality show—but they cared about the money. Gambling. Food carts. Rewards for scouting new animals. Or low-level work at NuFormz itself. It was already pretty hard to survive in the Drain, and thanks to Leesa, half the economy had just collapsed.

They hated her.

"Come on," Leesa's mom whispered, pulling Leesa close to her. There were jeers as they wove through the main underground cavity where the population was most dense, but when they splintered off into the side tunnel that led to their section of an old subway car, people left them alone.

Safely inside their apartment, Leesa expected the feeling of victory to really set in. Regardless of what anyone else wanted, she knew she had done what was right! She had changed things, *really* changed things for the better.

Only . . .

Here, inside their cramped apartment, it didn't feel like anything had changed. She was still poor, and her dad was still gone, and Pookie was still dead. Instead of some explosion of happiness filling her up, mostly, Leesa just felt kind of empty.

It seemed like a hundred years had gone by since she'd stepped aboveground to meet Marcus on the bridge and come up with a plan to free the animals. She had seen how big the sky was, and how high the towers. She had seen how the rich lived, with their windows and their space. She had met the mayor. But that wasn't her life.

"I have to go back to work," her mom said.

Leesa nodded and slumped down onto their shared sofa bed. "I know."

Her mom was always working—that hadn't changed, either. After running errands for rich sky snobs during the day, she had the night shift at one of the synthi factories. Even without the added debt from the damages in the Dome, would they ever have enough money to get out of the Drain?

"I'm so sorry, Mom," Leesa said. Despite helping the animals like she'd always dreamed, there was still so much wrong in the world. Leesa felt like crying.

"Oh, lovebug." Her mom bent down to give Leesa a hug. "No matter what, I'm proud of you. You know that, right? You know your heart, Leesa," her mom said. "That's all I could ever ask for."

Once her mom left, Leesa was restless. She wished she was back at street level for just a minute, so she could see what the talking heads were saying. Every major news outlet was sure to be streaming onto the buildings. She wondered if there had been any information about the escaped animals, or about what would happen to all the other mutants on the island at NuFormz.

She picked up her ratty old tablet. It was too outdated to mindscroll like Marcus's simulink, but it could still access the main news sources.

Leesa saw that irrational fear had taken hold of Lion's Head. A lot of the citizens had assumed the mutants were just virtual or robotics, but now that the mayor had said they were real, violent animals, people were freaking out. A lot of the headlines speculated about the mayor's suggestion of a corrupt employee, and she wondered about what Joni had said about a serum, but there wasn't any more information.

She tried to text Marcus to see what he knew, but his name wasn't lit on her screen. Leesa assumed he was grounded from simulink—his stepdad seemed pretty strict.

Leesa took the stolen book from her pocket. It had a girl on the cover, holding a strange glass circle thing on a stick. The text said her name was Nancy Drew. Leesa loved reading—it was the only thing that kept her going back to school—but books were pretty rare in the Drain. Of course a sky girl would have a whole shelfful.

When Leesa opened the book, she was struck by the writing on the inside. It was weird to see the script, because Leesa had never really learned to write using a pen—they were so outdated.

To Francine, the note read. *I hope this brings you comfort as you go through this. Reading is a wonderful escape throughout the trials of our lives. Even if we cannot get out of bed, adventure can come to us! Be well, Ms. Hoiles.*

Leesa started. Ms. Hoiles was Leesa's teacher, who had first introduced her to books. Ms. Hoiles knew the mayor's daughter, Francine, too?

The wheels in Leesa's mind were already turning. Francine loved animals, and the mayor had said she'd do anything for Francine. Maybe if Leesa could get to Francine, together they could turn around the treatment of the mutants and really make a change. And now she had a connection!

20

First, success had only looked like a tiny circle of light. But Samken kept pummeling the walls, and Enza kept scratching at the stone, and Castor kept digging around the pipes, and finally, Jazlyn gave the ceiling a good, strong kick—and the circle widened into an exit as the pavement above them collapsed in.

"Wow," Castor heard his friends saying as they climbed up. "Unbelievable."

The eagle-dog had been the last to jump into the hole

in the middle of the arena, and now he was the last to step out of the hole in the street. He swayed a little on his four legs. Castor was the only one of the group who had ever been outside before—really outside, not in an enclosed zoo or a temperature-controlled aquarium— yet he was more overwhelmed than anyone by the sight of the city.

His city: Lion's Head.

He felt almost as he had the first time he'd stepped into the Dome, with his senses going haywire. The sun was so bright, like a white-hot metal coin shining over-head. The heat was so extreme, like a great big tongue licking his fur. The smells were so varied, from garbage, to smoke, to diesel.

It was almost too much, and Castor was dizzy. He had to remind himself this wasn't like the ring. This was *home*. Here, he had nothing to fear.

"Um, Castor?" Jazlyn said. "We should probably get going."

He followed her gaze upward. The dark glass tow-ers rose up all around them, and on their sides flashed hundreds of images. Castor had grown up watching these images change—he had even learned to read from staring at the jumbles of text. Castor remembered see-ing advertisements and news stories. It was where he'd first seen Laringo's face, where he'd first heard about the Unnaturals reality show.

Back then, he hadn't had any idea how *real* reality could be.

Now, instead of all sorts of different images streaming onto the windows, there were just four: one of Samken, one of Jazlyn, one of Enza, and one of him. He recognized the images right away as the publicity posters Mega Media had used to promote this season's Unnaturals teams. Each image took up a full side of a building—in the picture of him, Castor's wings seemed to be touching the sun. The text read: "Fugitives. Extremely dangerous. Contact the mayor's office with any information."

"We need to figure out which way the Greenplains are," Enza said.

Jazlyn disagreed. "First we need to find someplace safe."

Castor had not planned to go home. He had told himself he couldn't go back there. But now that it was so close, he felt its pull. Besides, it was the best option.

"I know a place."

Castor was surprised at how natural it felt to run in these streets again. He barely felt the weight of his wings. His talons were dull enough that they barely scraped on the pavement. He felt like a dog again.

Or at least he thought that he felt like a dog, until he rounded the last corner. At the end of the alley, the pack of dogs froze. Even from a block away, he recognized his old family—the bulldogs, Pittie Paula, Alpha. But they didn't seem to recognize him. They were standing defensively. Their shoulders were squared off, their tails pointing out straight behind them. As he got closer, he could see the fur on their backs standing up. He noticed the flash of teeth.

"What's wrong?" asked Samken. "Castor, why are they looking at us like that? Like we're Laringo or something."

The dogs were uncertain, anxious. More than that, they were scared. Castor could smell their fear.

He had grown up with these dogs. He had slept in a messy pile with them in the shade every afternoon. He had hunted rats with them in the darkness. He had fought alongside them in territory battles. Yet they did not know him.

"It's me," Castor called out.

Some of the dogs started to shift their weight a little. Their ears perked up, and some of their tails started to wag tentatively. "Castor?"

"This is Enza. And Jazlyn. And Samken." Castor looked back at his team. "And this is . . . my pack."

"*My* pack," Alpha corrected. The boxer stepped forward and puffed out his chest.

Castor bristled. He had been beaten and almost broken at the NuFormz center. His whole life had been a set of rules. But despite all that the humans had done to him there, Castor had commanded a certain amount of respect. It had been a long time since he'd hung his head. A long time since he'd begged for anything. From anyone.

But they didn't have many other options right now.

Castor lowered himself into a crouch, the fur of his belly brushing along the dusty ground. He crawled toward Alpha. He could feel his teammates' eyes on him, the questions they were holding back. *Was this who Castor had been before? Is this who he would become once again?*

"Alpha, we beg your mercy," Castor said through gritted teeth.

Alpha looked down at him for a beat too long, until it seemed like he really might turn them away. But Castor could feel the excitement of the other dogs, too. It would be bad for morale if their long-lost brother was exiled. They would think Alpha was afraid. They would lose respect for him. Alpha knew this, too, of course. Finally, he pushed his lower jaw forward. "Fine," he huffed. "I,

Alpha, grant you conditional asylum."

"Conditional?" Enza cut in, narrowing her golden eyes. The grizzly stood on her hind legs, rising to her full, towering height. "What is that supposed to mean?"

"It means I decide," Alpha said, not backing down. "Here, I decide everything."

The mutants advanced down the alley. Castor couldn't believe he was back in his old den. There was the gutter he had played in, the familiar crack in the concrete where the sun had baked it. The bulldogs, and the hounds, and the lab mixes. *Home.*

"Where's Runt?" Castor asked. He didn't see his little brother anywhere. "Is he out hunting?"

The other dogs glanced at each other, uneasy.

"What is it?" Castor asked.

"He . . . Runt went after you," Brenda, one of the bulldog triplets, answered. "Just a few days ago. He kept going on about you having to fight some scorpion-cat thing. He was really worried about it. Said he was going to go save you."

"Always was a dumb mutt," Alpha said, and it took every bit of self-control Castor had to keep from lunging for his throat.

21

KOZMO WAS SURPRISED AT HOW COMFORTABLE SHE FELT IN the tunnels. She loved their darkness and their solitude. She loved how the walls hugged close around her; they were like the den she'd wished she had all those days in the room. Maybe this was what the dog had meant by *home*.

The tunnels were teeming with life. In the walls, she found efficient colonies of termites, building tiny cities out of rotting wood. In the ground, she found worms, making their journeys through the mud. There were rats, too, and she saw the flash of their red eyes hidden between the tracks. And there were things that looked like *her*—or at least the part of her with wings—hanging upside down from the curved beams. When she got near them, though, they took flight, squeaking as they flapped away.

Kozmo had never minded being alone. The other mutants seemed closer to machines than animals, so she had never craved their company. But out here, where the world was so *different* but the other beings were something that felt familiar—more like her—she felt, for the first time, lonely.

She wanted . . . what had the dog called them?

Friends.

"Kozmo," she whispered shyly to herself, repeating the name Runt had given her. "My friends call me Kozmo."

It took days before she picked up on any echoing signals from the dog and the lizard. Then, one night, when Kozmo was digging for worms in the soft clay earth of the tunnel, she heard something that sounded like more than the *shhhh shhhh* of wormy bodies sliding through the dirt. Kozmo's ears twitched as she focused on isolating the direction, and when she let out a screech, she detected a warm, sleeping body off a turn in the railroad tracks.

She crept along the track, slinking low, with her wings pulled in tight and tail straight out behind her.

When she came upon them, Kozmo almost let out a squeaky giggle. Runt was sprawled, belly up, and his paws were twitching as if he was dreaming. Every few breaths he let out a little yip, as if he were giving chase. The lizard lay curled up beside him with its chin tucked into the dog's neck—they seemed more like two pups than a cold-blooded amphibian and a warm-blooded mammal.

As excited as she was to finally find them, Kozmo decided to hang back at a safe distance and study them for a while. During the day, whenever she wasn't sleeping, Kozmo tracked the pair by hiding in narrow crevices in the ceiling and crawling in the ditches between train tracks. At night, she would use echoes to locate them and catch up to them in darkness.

Runt seemed harmless enough, and she knew he hadn't received the shot yet, but she knew little about the lizard. She knew it smelled tropical and had some blue goo on its scales, which made her wonder if it had harmed the human girl in the room. But Kozmo also knew it had saved her.

Why isn't that enough?

Kozmo told herself that she wanted to understand these creatures better on her own terms—it definitely had nothing to do with worrying that they would reject her.

Runt chattered on endlessly, and at top volume. Kozmo could be trailing them by a quarter mile, and she could still learn about his home (Trash mountains! So smelly and delicious!), and his pack (Alpha hates me but lil Esmerelda loves me but the wee weenies try to fight us all!), and his brother (Castor the eagle-dog, Underdog, shepherd dog, winner, can you help me find him, please!).

The lizard, on the other paw, seemed to be always changing. On the first day, it stepped gingerly as it walked, lifting up its feet with each muddy step and placing them with great effort one in front of the other. Kozmo wondered if it had been in a cage for so long that it had forgotten how to walk. At night, it lay strangely on its side, its tail curled up around it, shivering. Its skin was a bright, glowing green—a sharp contrast to the earthy walls around it—and it was sure to be a target for any predator they encountered.

The lizard was an excellent mimic, though, and by the third night, things had changed. The lizard was scuttling up the walls, and its body had turned a muddy gray to match its surroundings. It wriggled under Runt while he slept, absorbing the heat from the dog's heavy pelt.

It didn't speak much at first, so Runt called it Flicker after its flicking tongue and tail. But one day Kozmo heard excited barking and she heard the lizard making sounds, too—high, soft, rhythmic sounds—and though Kozmo could understand their talk of adventure and escape, the accent scared her a little bit.

Besides, they called each other best friend, and Kozmo realized she didn't know much about how a friend should act. So far, it looked like a friend was someone to laugh with, and imagine adventures with, and curl up against when you were cold, which seemed nice.

But, Kozmo wondered, *can you have more than one friend?*

And would someone want to be your friend if you had almost attacked them in a pen one time to prove to people that you were tough and not different from anyone else in the Room?

Or is that to be expected?

Kozmo decided she had better hang back a bit longer, you know, just to be sure.

22

CASTOR WAS SURPRISED BY HOW LITTLE HAD CHANGED IN the alley. The streets looked exactly the same, smelled the same. It was hard to believe that while he was in that lab, his body becoming a whole new creature, and then later when each day was life or death in the Dome, everything had just continued as usual for the pack. They still worried about the same territory scuffles. They still made fun of Chauncy Chow and his pack of wee weenies. They still bickered over the fattest rats and the shadiest spot to sleep. They still deferred to Alpha's pointless bullying.

From the moment he'd been taken away, Castor had longed to return to this place, this normalcy. He was surprised to find that now, normal felt strange.

When he left, Castor had known his place in the pack. He was not an alpha, not an omega, but somewhere in between. He was a reliable scavenger and a better hunter. The old dogs liked him because he listened to their stories, the young pups appreciated that he'd never snitch to Alpha, and everyone knew he could be counted on to defend the territory.

Now, his place was uncertain, and none of the pack knew how to treat him. Some tried to pretend that he was the same old shepherd dog he'd always been.

"Castor, wanna go for a hunt?" Esmerelda, one of the hound pups, asked him, baring her teeth fiercely.

"Castor, come join the pile," Winky, a friend of Runt's, offered, making room for him on the outer edges of the sleeping spot, a space that would've been far below his station before.

He couldn't go striding through the streets of Lion's Head in search of raccoons anymore, though—not with his face plastered on every Sky Tower. And he couldn't seem to get comfortable in the pile, either, since every time a dog shifted, his wings got squashed and his feathers bent.

There were other dogs who treated him like a freak. They wanted all the grisly details of NuFormz, or they thought he had special powers, or they acted like his wings were some kind of gift to the pack.

"What is it?" he asked BipBip, one of the bulldog triplets he'd noticed sniffing around.

"It's just . . . You smell kind of like chicken." Bip eyed Castor's feathers longingly, and a string of drool spilled out of the side of his jowls. He licked his chops. "Can I just have a little lick?"

"No, you cannot lick my wings!" Castor barked. "Scram!"

Then there were the dogs who didn't seem excited about his return at all, including Alpha. They were even less welcoming of Castor's new friends. They said Samken was too big, and Enza was too hostile. And if Jazlyn hadn't been so quick, they would've considered her food. There was also the fact that they *actually* couldn't fit here. Samken could barely turn around in the alley. When the rains came and the whole pack crowded under a sheet of plastic, Castor stood outside, shielding the other mutants with his wings.

Alpha complained that it was a burden on the pack to shelter fugitives, so to pull their weight, Castor and his teammates ventured farther and farther into the trash mountains. The dump was crawling with Crusher Slushers, machines that churned garbage—and everything else—into sludge, but they had few options.

There wasn't any shelter big enough for Samken, and the octo-elephant was the only one capable of destroying a Crusher Slusher thanks to his tanklike body, so he stood guard. The long nights took their toll, though, and most days, Samken shuffled around wearily, dazed and depressed.

"Why are we here?" Enza asked Castor after a week. "When are we going to the Greenplains?"

"Soon," Castor promised. "Really soon."

But as strained as things were with the pack, Castor still wasn't ready to leave. He wanted to go to the Greenplains more than anything, he told himself. He just needed a little more time to recuperate. To settle in. To remember what *home* felt like.

23

One afternoon, Castor was on the outer edge of the territory, digging for edible trash, when he heard a rustling behind him.

"Jazz, check this out," he said. "I found a book all about biology, just like in your old classroom!"

But when Castor turned around, it wasn't Jazlyn behind him. He recognized the beagle with the nicked ear right away, and the mean-mugged Dalmatian. It was the pack he and Runt had fought the day he was taken. It made no sense that they were on this side of town. Normally, a northside pack couldn't get a few feet into the southeast territory before some dog sounded the alarm.

So where was his pack?

"A little mouse told us you were back in town. We've been waiting for you a long time. Time to settle the score."

The dogs surrounded him. He'd fought these dogs before, but back then, there had been eight, maybe ten of them. Now there had to be thirty—the entire pack. Castor was not just outnumbered. He was dead meat.

And, pushed up against a mound of garbage, he was cornered.

The only advantage Castor had was flight. He pushed off the ground and snapped open his wings. He pumped the muscles hard, gaining air with every downstroke.

Boy, it felt good to fly. He dove and soared to stretch his wings. He did some barrel rolls and loops for old times' sake, remembering his training with his mentor, Pookie.

"You are not only dog anymore," Pookie had told him once. "You are bird and dog, one and the same."

Castor never thought he'd grow to *like* being a mutant, and he certainly didn't miss his matches in the Dome, but he did miss this part—the wind whipping through his tail feathers, the precision of a hairpin turn, the escape when you were out of reach of everything else. With all the running and hiding and cowering, this was the first time he'd felt a true sense of freedom since he'd left the chains behind.

The wind was whipping so fast in his ears that Castor didn't even hear the sound of the propeller at first. He only noticed the flying machine when a blue light—some kind of laser—flashed into his eyes. He'd been spotted!

Castor needed to warn his friends, but the machine trailed him closely. It looked like a fat bumblebee, with oval wings and a buzzing propeller. But instead of a bee's fuzzy body, a heavy metal sphere cage hung between the wings. The two halves of the cage locked together like jaws, and they opened and closed, opened and closed, snapping at the air and hoping to catch something good.

Like an eagle-dog.

It was right on his tail, its metal jaws going *chomp chomp, chomp chomp*. It was too quick in the air—if Castor wanted to lose it, he had to swoop low.

The problem was, he had been away for so long that he didn't know the newest trails of the trash mountains, and though he was trying to confuse the machine's signals, Castor himself ended up turned around, and when he turned a corner, the enemy dog pack was there waiting for him.

In a last ditch effort to send the flying machine off course and confuse the dogs, Castor stopped, dropped, and rolled into a pile of garbage to his left. The buzzing just got louder, though, and the propeller chopped through the trash, seeking out its target. As paper and food scraps fluttered around him, Castor glimpsed Enza leaping at the machine, swiping with her big bear claws.

The metal bee wasn't even dented, and as Enza continued to attack, the cage wrenched open and closed on a tight spring, swallowing up the huge saber-toothed grizzly like a Venus flytrap.

Samken was charging toward it now.

"Stay away from it!" Castor barked a warning. "There's no killing it. No hurting it, even."

But Samken had wrapped his eight trunks around a wing, anyway, and was slamming the machine against the ground hoping to bust it open to free their friend. The metal jaws didn't budge, but a mechanical claw did spring out of the top. It snapped around Samken's wispy tail and dangled the many-tonned octo-elephant upside down as it started to buzz off.

"No!"

Castor flapped after it, and Jazlyn raced along below. But though she was fast, Jazlyn was tired, and Castor could see the enemy pack closing in from the outsides, waiting for her to stumble.

"Don't follow us, Castor," Samken cried. "You have to get away."

"We're a team!" Castor insisted. But to make matters worse, he heard another buzz as a second trapping machine flew up over the trash mountain to the south of them. Soon he wouldn't have a choice.

"Get to the Greenplains, shepherd dog," Enza's voice commanded through the holes of the flying metal sphere. "You have to carry the dream. You see that chance, and you jump for it!"

"I'll come back for you," he promised them. "We'll find a safe passage, and wherever you are, we'll find you. We'll see you in the Greenplains!"

"See you there," Samken said with a weak smile. "Now go help my Jazz, and tell her Sammie's sorry he couldn't say good-bye."

Castor flew close enough to clasp one of Samken's trunk tentacles in his paw, and then he swooped down, grabbed Jazlyn in his talons, and flapped harder than he'd ever flapped.

He spotted a Crusher Slusher up ahead, but it was lying on its side, busted up. Castor never thought he'd be running *toward* a Crusher, but right now, it was their only hope.

24

CASTOR AND JAZLYN STAYED HIDDEN INSIDE THE BELLY OF the old Crusher Slusher. For a while, Castor was sure the machine would spring to life, that its gears would start grinding and it would crunch them up. He'd seen it happen to other animals. After a Crusher Slusher got a hold of you, all that was left behind was sludge.

He didn't hear anything stirring inside the machine, though. He couldn't hear anything at all, actually. For all the commotion earlier, now the world was reduced to the sound of their breath, still coming quick in the darkness, and the feel of Jazlyn shivering next to him.

"Where do you think they took them?" Jazlyn whispered. "Samken and Enza?"

Castor hung his head and slumped against the sidewall. He was afraid to imagine. Based on his past experiences, he knew that things could be worse than you might think. A lot worse. That was what kept him crouched inside this awful machine—the only thing scarier than knowing he could be turned into soup was not knowing *what* could happen.

Because deep down inside, Castor knew the truth about himself.

"I'm such a coward," he howled. His voice was low, but in the tight space the word seemed to grow.

"You are not," Jazlyn protested. "I saw you fight Laringo. I saw you rescue those kids. That was brave—even Pookie said so."

"You were brave, too."

"I know," Jazlyn said, surprising him. "We were all brave, Castor. We never would've escaped if we weren't."

Maybe that was true. But it was in the past. It didn't seem to count for much in their current circumstances.

"I just let them take my friends away. I did nothing." Castor was disgusted with himself.

"You saved me," Jazlyn said softly. "That wasn't nothing."

"Then I *hid*." And here he was, still hiding.

Jazlyn didn't say anything for a long time. Castor worried he'd hurt her feelings—after all, she had hid, too. But when she finally spoke, her voice was thoughtful, measured.

"I think that sometimes, hiding is its own kind of bravery."

Castor scoffed. "You met the dogs in my pack. Not one of them would've backed down from a fight. Not one of them would've just turned tail and run."

"And not one of them has lived as a mutant, persecuted by the city's most powerful humans," Jazlyn countered. "Think of Pookie, waiting in the wings and coming up with a smart strategy. Or Moss, sacrificing his own freedom to help humans, when humans had beaten him down his whole life."

She didn't point out that not one of the dogs had shown up to help, either, but of course he had noticed that, too.

"Look, Castor. Before, back at NuFormz, we didn't have much to lose. We were already miserable, and every day we stayed there, we knew something terrible might happen. Leaving might have been scary, but it was an easy choice. Now, decisions are harder. We have everything to lose."

"What we had was our team. And we just lost it!"

"Stop it," Jazlyn snapped, her body tensing. Castor was surprised to hear a sharpness in her voice. "You don't think I feel awful? Enza was captured because she was defending me. And Samken is my best friend. But there was no way we could've protected them. What we *can* protect is our freedom. Stop acting like that's worthless."

Jazlyn scooted away from him, and though he couldn't see her face, Castor could feel the tension between them. He'd spent plenty of time bickering with Enza and challenging Moss when they'd trained as a team, but things had always been easy between Castor and Jazlyn. She'd always been on his side, until now.

Before he could respond, there was a rap on the side of the machine. *Boom, boom, boom* echoed inside, and Castor flinched.

Is this it? Is it over?

Castor couldn't imagine that if the humans had really come for them, they'd have the manners to knock. He crept to the front, nudged open the door with his nose, and peered out. The coast was clear. There was not a human or a flying claw in sight. There was only Pitbull

Paula, one of the toughest members of the pack. Her ears were pulled back, and she looked impatient.

"Alpha wants to see you," Pittie Paula said, without so much as a wag of the tail to say she was glad Castor was all right. "Now."

Castor climbed out of the Crusher Slusher, and Jazlyn hopped out after him. They must've been inside for a long time, because night had already fallen. Castor arched his back and stretched out his back legs, his muscles crampy from sitting in one spot for so long. It had been a long, terrible day, and all he really wanted to do was get some sleep. But Alpha was waiting.

Pittie Paula trotted ahead, weaving her way through the hills and valleys of the trash mountains. Castor tried to keep pace, but he had to step gingerly so his talons wouldn't snag on the many objects that littered the ground, and he found himself constantly scanning the black sky overhead, on guard for another attack. Jazlyn hung back even farther.

When they reached the dead-end alley, the other dogs were all sitting in a circle. The pack elders huddled together on one side, corralling a jumble of new pups, and the bulldogs flanked Alpha. Everyone looked up as the pitbull approached with Castor and Jazlyn in tow. No one looked particularly happy to see them.

"The pack has to move," Alpha announced. "We have to go in search of new territory."

"But it's not you they're after."

"Does it matter? Have you been off the streets so long you've forgotten the risks? These streets are crawling with Crusher Slushers waiting to grind us up and turn us into sludge. More dogs disappear off the streets every day."

"If the humans come back—"

"*When* they come back, we will all have to pay your debt."

"Fine," Castor agreed. "We should move."

"Perhaps we should move in one direction, and you should move in another."

The suggestion hit Castor in the gut. But many others in the pack were surprised, too. They started to growl and bark in protest.

"You put us at risk."

"I stand with Castor."

"Me too. He is still our brother."

Alpha hadn't been challenged, for as long as Castor could remember. He was stronger than Alpha now, and he was an experienced leader. Now was his chance to challenge Alpha, to become head of the pack.

He could tell the others felt that way, too. They were

looking at him, waiting for him to step up. But then Pittie Paula spoke up.

"Just you, though, Castor." She sniffed Jazlyn dismissively. "A cat was never part of this pack, and neither was a rodent. Certainly not something that's half of each."

"Jazlyn is not some*thing*," Castor snapped. "She's some*one*."

But it didn't matter what she was. Castor could see that the rest of his supporters agreed with Paula. They were willing to stand by him, but only if he walked away from Jazlyn. His heart sank.

Jazlyn's eyes met his. Despite their earlier argument, there was no resentment in her look now, only warmth. She smiled at him, gave a little nod, her long ears flopping forward. Castor knew she was telling him it was okay, that she would be fine on her own. She wouldn't hold it against him.

In his heart, Castor knew there was only one clear choice. He had to be true to what he was. He had to stand by his family.

And that was Jazlyn, regardless of her DNA.

Castor had thought he could just come home, that he could go back to his old life. But Pookie turned out to be right: he was not a dog anymore. He had not been a dog for a long time. The only way he could know how to live now was to stay true to who he was *inside*. And what made him Castor was his loyalty, his honor.

The dogs were asking him to choose, but Jazlyn had never asked him for anything. She had been there for him since the first day they met, when she shared her water with a scared, thirsty stranger. She had been a friend even when he didn't want or deserve one. Now he felt closer to her than almost anyone—even these dogs he'd known his whole life.

"Okay," Castor said. "We'll leave in the morning. I wish Alpha and his supporters luck in their search for a new territory." Pitbull Paula started to move toward Castor, and Alpha growled, ready to fight to keep control of the whole pack. But Castor turned his back on them both and went to stand by the rabbit-panther's side. "Jazlyn and I will head to the Greenplains. Together."

25

MARCUS FELT LIKE A POT SET TO BOIL. THERE WAS NO word from Pete, no contact with Leesa, and no news about the Unnaturals. Add to that the fact that he was grounded and stuck in his room, and he was ready to scream. Not that outside his room was any better—his mom was a wreck trying to figure out what was going on with Pete.

Marcus's room was stocked full of gadgets and toys, but with the slipstream cut and the Unnaturals matches done, most of his tech was pretty useless. He was sick of the dumb automopooch his parents had gotten him, and there were only so many times he could watch his skateboarding videos before wanting to chuck his own board at the wall. He actually ended up doing all his homework, for once.

And then he started looking out the window.

With the other towers packed so close together, Marcus had a pretty good view of the changing ad and news streams that broadcast along the buildings. Until now, he'd mostly considered them neon white noise, a constant flicker in his peripheral vision, but nothing to really pay attention to. But now that he didn't have his simulink to look up anything he wanted, they were pretty much his only connection to the outside world.

Before, in his Moniac days, Marcus had sat in his highly coveted warp throne and virtually attended dozens of Unnaturals matches. Now, he scooted the chair right up close to the window, spun it to face the buildings, and stared out at the city. For hours and hours.

He saw smog warnings, and SunLife ads, and a preview for some new virtual show to hook all the old Moniacs who were missing the Unnaturals. Then he saw the Unnaturals themselves.

It was the Fearless and the Enforcer, being carried

away in an auto-hele.

Captured!

Marcus pressed his nose against the glass, but the video loop didn't show whether the Underdog and the Swift had been picked up, too. His heart dropped down to his stomach. Lion's Head had been on lockdown since the escape, and the animals' pictures were plastered everywhere. He knew that half the city was out looking for them.

But he still couldn't believe it. After everything they'd done, how could the escape just fail?

Then he saw a headline scrolling across Cloud Tower: *Mayor Agrees to a Sit-Down-Tell-All with Ex-Matchmaker Joni Juniper—Watch Now on Free101!*

Marcus instinctively signaled for the simulink at his temple before remembering he was grounded. Then he sprinted out of his room and down the hall.

"Mom!" he yelled. "I need the slipstream password just for a sec. It's really import—"

"Shh!" Marcus's mom held a finger to her lips. She was standing in the living room with tense shoulders and wide eyes, already watching the interview.

Marcus went to join her. It felt comforting standing there with her, close but not touching, and he was relieved Bruce was working late.

It was a nonsponsor channel, so the quality wasn't great, but Marcus saw Mayor Eris and Joni Juniper sitting and facing one another. It wasn't a true face-to-face—they were using avatars—but it was still pretty impressive Joni had landed the interview. Since the mayor owned Mega Media, she probably didn't want to give clicks to one of the other big streams.

"Why not resume the matches?" Joni was asking. "You've still got a lot of Moniacs out there who will be very disappointed to lose the Unnaturals."

Why is she acting like it was a bad thing that the matches are over? Marcus knew Joni didn't believe in the matches. She was Pete's girlfriend, and she was the one who'd told him to help Marcus and Leesa with the escape. Maybe it was to get clicks from her old fans. Or to gain the mayor's trust.

"As I said earlier, safety is our number one priority. The Unnaturals have had a good run, but we cannot risk these creatures terrorizing the city. Fortunately, thanks to the excellent work of our force, some of the escaped animals were apprehended today."

"Can you tell us what will become of these creatures, now that they are no longer contestants?" Joni asked.

"Many fans are quite concerned about their well-being."

"I'm pleased to report that they will begin a new life in the Greenplains, where we have a resettlement program in the early stages."

Marcus stared at the mayor's smiling avatar. *Is she serious? Are the animals really going to go free in the jungle?*

"There are those who question your prohibiting access to the NuFormz island with so many questions still lingering about what went wrong that tragic night at the arena."

"The facility is being evacuated," Mayor Eris said, her voice rising a hair. "You can tell *some people* that Mega Media will certainly cooperate with any investigation. But it's essential that we protect the citizens from these extremely dangerous mutants."

"You hinted at one of your employees having a specific connection to the public endangerment. Can you comment on that?"

"Yes. The perpetrator is actually now in custody, as we have uncovered footage of the offense."

An image of a man popped up on the screen. He was sticking the Vicious with a large needle. Even with the poor quality, Marcus recognized his brother right away.

He heard his mom inhale sharply next to him, and

her hand flew up to cover her mouth.

Joni was visibly shocked and flustered. "W-what is Pe—this man—accused of?"

"Mega Media is filing charges of animal cruelty, endangerment, terrorism, and destruction of property," Mayor Eris answered. "Peter Lund was entrusted with caring for the animals, but he was actually torturing them, giving them a shot that would make them further evolve into killing machines."

"Sounds like a pretty scientifically advanced drug," Joni said, recovering. Now she was on the offensive. "Was this a steroid? A virus? And how would an intern get his hands on something so dangerous? What might be his motives?"

The mayor took a sip of water. "Well, Joni, I myself couldn't imagine. However, as I'm sure you know, there is an unfortunate culture of betting surrounding the matches. We at Mega Media do not condone the practice. Some in the media have speculated that this employee was a compromised individual, and we can only speculate that it was a way for him to make money. Unfortunately, it could be part of what led to the disaster in the arena."

"Part of? Are we to assume that there is further corruption inside the NuFormz facility?" Joni asked, her eyes flashing.

Mayor Eris gave a tight-lipped smile. "This single man is the only responsible party. He put our entire city at grave risk, and also let children into off-limits parts of the facility, endangering their lives. I'm thankful to put this whole unfortunate episode behind us."

Marcus was horrified. So Pete was in jail!

The mayor was diverting attention away from the real horrors going on at NuFormz by framing Pete for some sort of gambling thing. And now that she'd been forced to shut down the Unnaturals, somehow *she* was going to look like a hero!

Marcus knew this mess was all his fault. He had to figure out a way to free Pete, but he knew he couldn't do it on his own. His mom had collapsed onto the couch, and she was staring into space, shaking her head back and forth. She wasn't going to be any help right now, and obviously neither was Bruce.

Marcus grabbed his mom's device, checked into his slipstream, and looked up two contacts. He typed in three letters and quickly sent the message to Leesa, and then to Joni: *SOS*.

PART TWO

FOXES AND HOUNDS

"Fall of a Franchise and an Unnatural Unraveling"

"In a City Under Siege, Can Eris Lead?"

"The Mystery of Peter Lund: Where Is He?"

26

Back in the beginning, you learn to fly. You have no mother now, no littermates, so you learn to do it alone.

You squint with your poor eyesight, and you climb onto the tallest thing you can find, a lab stool, inching yourself up. You jump off and crash to the floor, crumpling into a fox-bat heap on the linoleum. You hear laughter from the other cages, but you do it again, again.

Finally, you learn to jump up instead of out, and you learn to flap quickly instead of steadily. You climb into the air this time before you fall. And the next time you do it you flail for a half a second longer.

Your hunger makes you stupid, and your flapping scares away all the bugs. But eventually, you learn to trust your voice, your wings, your muscles.

"Food?" you call out, and the sound loops back to you with information. It seems to say, "Right here!" and a firefly zips into your mouth with a pop.

The darkness feels like it has layers as you dip and dive through it, and though your eyesight is bad, you see blue, and orange, and white streaks as you sense the heat of other creatures around you. The world makes sense.

Your instincts are so good, you begin to believe you can't miss.

Sometimes, you still do. It is only when you think you know where you are going that you are deceived. The path changes, the prey migrates, a door is opened that was closed before. It is only when you expect routine that you falter.

You end up with a bump on your head, a torn wing, an empty stomach.

Trust your path, you start to remind yourself each night. Trust the layers in the darkness. Trust your instincts.

27

Castor and Jazlyn were back underground, back where they started on the train tracks, back on the path to the Greenplains. This felt like a new journey, though. It was deliberate—they weren't running blind anymore. Castor's eyes had never been more open.

Castor had thought that when his mentor died, his education would end. Pookie had been so old, and he'd seen so much of the world, that Castor didn't think he could learn more from anyone else. But the first new thing he had learned was that, it turned out, lots of different creatures could teach you about the world, even when they didn't know they were doing it. They could show you the kind of dog you wanted to be . . . and, just as importantly, the kind you didn't.

Now, Jazlyn was padding along by his side in the musky gloom, matching him step for step, and Castor didn't doubt that he'd chosen the right path.

"Thank you," she said quietly. "For what you did back there. Leaving with me."

Castor stopped in his tracks. "You don't have to thank me for being your friend, Jazz."

"I just know it must've been hard, is all, to walk away from your family." Her voice trailed off as she loped ahead of him into the darkness.

"Hey." Castor gave Jazlyn's tail a tug so she would turn around. "*They* walked away from *me*. From us. You're my family now."

Jazlyn's nose twitched a little uncertainly, but her eyes were bright. "Yeah?"

Castor nudged past her, giving her a playful bump with his shoulder. "Yeah."

"I think I just purred."

"Do panthers purr?"

"They do now!" Jazlyn laughed. "Maybe I really am

still evolving."

That's what the news on the buildings had said—Castor had read the headlines just before they disappeared below. He and Jazlyn fell silent thinking of the images that went with those headlines: 3D video of their friends being captured. For Castor, it was almost worse to watch the second time, when he wasn't terrified and running for his life. He could really see Enza's anger as she swiped at the metal that gripped her, and from the way Samken's body went slack, he seemed devastated.

"It's so quiet without Samken," Jazlyn said after a few minutes.

"I know. And who will insult me now that Enza's gone?"

"I could try. Your growl is not as mean as you think, Underdog!"

Castor barked a laugh. "Still too nice."

"Do you think they really made it to the Green-plains?"

That was what the ads said. But with the humans and their brightly projected reality, how could you know what was real?

"Definitely!" Castor answered, anyway. If he could say it, maybe he could believe it. "I bet if we speed it up, we can probably see them before nightfall. We'll all have a feast together under the stars and sleep on a soft bed of grass."

"Hey, if you wanted me to go faster, all you had to do was say so!"

Jazlyn stretched her panther legs and kicked up a cloud of dust in front of him, and Castor was left panting after her, his tail wagging.

They went on like that for a while, until they saw light ahead. It wasn't quite direct sunlight—there was some sort of filter—but it wasn't the fluorescent glare of NuFormz, either.

"Maybe it's opening up to the outside!" Castor shouted.

A little farther, they started to see trees. They looked a little more limp and sickly than Castor had expected, with leaves that were more yellow than green and branches that sagged, but they were still *real trees.*

"Maybe it's the start of the Greenplains!" Jazlyn yelled, and surged forward even faster.

She didn't see that the track ended suddenly at a sharp drop-off until she was nearly there. Jazlyn put on the breaks, but she was going so fast her head and shoulders kept traveling, even as her legs skidded on the earth. The soft rocks at the edge broke away and fell, and Jazlyn was on her way to following them. Castor sprang forward and snatched her up with his talons.

"Gotcha!" he panted, yanking her back just before she went over the cliff.

It wasn't really a cliff, though—more of a crevasse. The earth dipped into a wide bowl below and a vast, round ceiling was carved overhead. It almost looked like the inside of the Dome, but underground. It was some kind of machine graveyard. Castor saw metal boxes with windows like he'd seen on the tracks before—Jazlyn called them subway cars—but this time, there were dozens of them stacked on top of one another, piled all the way to the ceiling, like makeshift buildings cobbled together. There were ladders and ropes climbing up them.

In the bottom of the bowl, there were little dirt paths snaking through the stacked metal cars, and more wilted plants. There were also carts like the ones in the Dome, with smells that made Castor drool, and tables laid out with colorful items and hand-drawn signs that reminded Castor of the window-lit images on the buildings in Lion's Head—advertisements for everything a human could want.

Oh, yeah, and there were humans. *Everywhere.* More humans than Castor had seen in the packed stands of the

Dome before a big match. More than he'd seen walking behind the glass in the towers. Probably more humans than Castor had seen all together in his lifetime.

And all it would take was for even *one* of them to glance up and see a certain most-wanted winged dog and a very conspicuous bunny-eared panther hanging out at a well-lit tunnel entrance, and their journey would be over, just like their friends'.

Jazlyn was shaking next to him, doing her signature bunny freeze. Castor had to tug her back into the tunnel by her long black tail before she snapped out of it. Then she was all business, rational as ever.

"We can backtrack," she suggested. "Go *over* the river instead of under."

"What about the flying bee things?" Castor said.

"Well, if you weren't carrying me, then you could probably outfly them, especially if you knew they were coming."

Castor cocked his head, confused. "If I wasn't carrying you, then we wouldn't be going to the Greenplains together."

"I mean, if you wanted to go by yourself I would understand," Jazlyn said, with a twitch of her pink nose. "Like Enza said, at least one of us should make it, and . . ."

"All of us are going to make it!" Castor barked. "First

166

you and me are going to get to the Greenplains together, and then we'll go back for the others. If I didn't abandon you for the dog pack, what makes you think I'm going to start now?"

Jazlyn's eyes softened, and she hopped over to him. "Thank you."

"You don't have to thank me for being your friend."

Jazlyn snickered. "That's what I said to you when we first met. Well, looks like we'd better find another tunnel, then. Maybe we should stay away from train tracks this time."

"Who cares about the tracks?" Castor said with a wry bark. "How about we just stay away from the humans?"

28

LEESA FELT WEIRD WALKING TOWARD THE JAIL. SHE KNEW her dad had been in there before—he might be in there now, for all she knew—but she'd never come to see him. Now she was here visiting some sky dude, and she couldn't help feeling guilty.

But whatever. Her dad was the reason her pet Chihuahua had become an Unnatural, while this sky dude had actually helped her free some of them. Pete was in here because he'd agreed to help her and Marcus when no one else would, not even her supposed best friend. Now it was their turn to help him.

Joni had kept her promise and was waiting at the entrance, and Leesa saw that Marcus was already standing next to her. She noticed he didn't have his arm sling anymore, or his skateboard. Leesa felt a weird little flutter when she saw him slouching there with his blond hair flopping over his left eye, looking way more relaxed than she felt and making her believe things would actually be fine somehow.

"Hey, look, it's the hero," he said, shrugging his hair off his brow to look at her. "You looked pretty cute in the publicity photo. The blue streak in your hair goes well with your scowl."

Even though he'd just said she looked cute, Leesa's flutter of affection turned to a twinge of annoyance. She knew he was going to be weird about not getting credit.

"I didn't know she was going to say that," Leesa said defensively. "I didn't even know there was going to be a press conference. She was just using me like she uses everyone else. Like she's using Pete."

"Whoa," Marcus said, laughing. "I was just giving you a hard time."

Leesa wasn't convinced, though. "Everyone in the Drain hates me now, by the way. Is that why you've been ignoring me, because you're mad you weren't the one she picked to blame?"

"I was grounded! Bruce even killed my simulink. I've pretty much spent the last week going crazy alone in my room."

"But your parents let you come here?" She squinted at him.

"No way. Bruce is at NuFormz helping to close down the center, and my mom is at her prayer group. I snuck out."

"Gutsy."

He shrugged, like it was the only option. The sky boy had come a long way, considering he had freaked out about being unsupervised at NuFormz for ten minutes the first time she'd met him.

"We need to get Pete out."

"Let's not get ahead of ourselves," Joni said, ushering them forward. "I don't even know if they're going to let us *in*. A journalist, maybe, but two kids?"

Marcus looked like he was about to say something about being called a kid, but he kept his mouth shut. They both knew Joni was their best shot.

Luckily, the guard on duty in Pete's block was a Moniac. Not even a Moniac—a *Joniac*. He recited ten of her signature phrases and had her sign like twenty match cards. The guy was her biggest fan. It was all pretty disgusting, but at least it got them in to see Pete.

Pete was in gray-blue prison-issue clothes, and he was in a cell away from the others, in the solitary wing. Like he had done something really bad.

When they got to his cell, Joni rushed forward, clasping the bars.

"Pete! Are you okay?" Joni asked, her voice breaking.

Joni acted like he was receiving super-bad treatment and everything, but after seeing the Unnaturals' cells back at NuFormz, Leesa thought he had it pretty good. There were no windows or anything, but he had a bed and didn't have to go to the bathroom in a corner of his cell, for example.

He had deep circles under his eyes and his face looked drawn, but otherwise he seemed all right.

Pete held Joni's hand through the bars, and Leesa suddenly felt very self-conscious about standing so close to Marcus. She tucked her hands into her pockets, and then felt even dumber, and pulled them back out.

Marcus didn't even notice, though. He was looking at Pete like he might start crying, and then he started apologizing over and over, gripping the bars of the cell like he was going to rip them off or something.

"Marcus, you didn't do this," Pete insisted firmly.

"The mayor did this," Joni said.

But Pete wasn't going to just dismiss it like that. "I did, too, though," he said. "I made choices, and I stand by them."

Leesa appreciated that, but it made her wonder, too. "Does that mean you stand by the shot?" she blurted out.

Marcus looked upset that she'd asked that, but wasn't that why they were here? They needed to find out the truth, and if Pete wasn't going to give it to them, then what was the point of any of it?

But Pete just seemed confused. "What's she talking about?" he asked, looking at Joni.

Joni showed him the picture. "This is floating around—I think probably distributed by Eris. The media's speculating that you were giving the mutants steroids for guaranteed gambling wins."

"Wow." Pete let out a low whistle. "That's creative."

"I knew you wouldn't give them shots," Marcus said, satisfied.

Pete shifted awkwardly. "Well, I did, but like, just since the Mega Mash-up. Some of the remaining animals were pretty banged up, and I agreed to administer medical treatment while I was being held for questioning. The Invincible wasn't responding . . ."

Marcus wasn't surprised about that, after seeing a

cement pole crush the scorpion-tiger.

"But the mayor and Bruce were convinced he could be revived. They had these vials of serum, and I figured it couldn't hurt to try and save him. It actually worked really well, causing a jolt to the system, so then I tried it on the Vicious, too. They seemed fine at first, but then they started to change."

"Change how?"

"Well, both animals had always been violent because of how Horace trained them, but this made their mouths foam, their eyes red. . . . Afterward, they just had this strange drive to attack. Vince was the only one who could pull them off me. He seems to have a way with them."

"That was the first time you'd seen the serum at NuFormz?"

"Yeah. I mean, they give all the animals a shot of serum to change them into mutants. But this was different. It was in Bruce's private lab, and I'm not usually allowed in there. But there were rows and rows and rows of them. Looked like they were planning to give them to a lot more animals than just those two."

"But then the mayor shut down the Unnaturals. They're supposedly dismantling NuFormz. Why would they be mass-producing this serum that makes animals crazy if they're going to release them into the Green-plains?"

Pete sighed and ran his hands through his hair—it had gotten pretty dirty during his time in the slammer, and it was sticking up in all directions.

"I don't know, but Bruce was acting super weird about my involvement. He's always bossing me around at work, but he was very clear about not talking to anyone about it."

"We're not just anyone!" Marcus sputtered. "And you're going to listen to Bruce?" He looked really hurt, and Leesa didn't blame him. They'd come all this way to get some answers so they could help, and now his brother was giving them the cold shoulder? Marcus leaned forward and whispered urgently, "Pete, it's us. It's *me!*"

"I know, Marcus, but I think this is bigger than the escape. I just don't want to get you mixed up in something I don't even understand until we know what we're dealing with. If the mayor's lying about the reason I'm in here, things are probably more serious than we think."

"We're *going* to get him out of here," Joni promised, squeezing Marcus's shoulder. "We just have to figure out what the bigger game is that the mayor's playing."

"Let me know when you find out, will you?" Pete said. "I don't much like being the pawn."

Leesa thought about the new book she'd been read-ing. The girl in it, Nancy, was always looking for clues. If they were going to get Pete out of jail, they were going to need something that proved the mayor was lying, and it wasn't really his fault.

"We need something concrete," she said. "Evidence."

"There is one more thing," Pete said. "I heard two of the researchers whispering about something called K-group. They stopped talking as soon as Bruce walked into the lab."

K-group. That sounded like a clue.

29

While tracking Runt and the lizard, Kozmo had observed that the pair was not very good at gathering food.

"I'm starving," Runt groaned. "You don't think there are any raccoons scurrying around down here, do you, Flicker? What I wouldn't give for a fat, juicy raccoon right now."

The lizard flicked out her tongue, making a sound of disgust.

"I know what you're thinking," Runt went on. "Rats! I know, I know, rats are delicious. The thing is, I always hunted rats with my brother. Rats are mean and sneaky. You really need two dogs to hunt rats, otherwise you wind up getting ambushed by a whole bunch of them, and you end up with chew marks all over your legs, see?" He stuck out his back leg for the lizard to see. "Those are from my first hunt without Castor."

Flicker gagged again. Of course mammals with fur didn't sound appetizing to her, like they did to Runt! Kozmo was willing to bet that the lizard would prefer some crunchy invertebrates or a delectable bug medley. Flicker didn't seem to hunt on her own, though—maybe she had forgotten how after being fed slop in the Room for a while.

Kozmo decided to share her bounty. One night, she found a whole nest of centipedes. She made four trips back and forth with a mouthful of wiggling bugs, but she knew it would be worth it to see their expressions of gratitude when they woke up.

Runt and Flicker seemed to sleep *forever*, so she thought they might need a little help.

"Hey!" she screeched. "Look what I brought you!"

Runt opened one eye. "Did you hear that, Flicker?"

The centipedes started running. There were so many

it looked like the floor was moving. But Runt and the lizard weren't jumping forward to gobble them up. Instead, they were just jumping straight into the air.

Soon both dog and lizard were shaking wildly.

Runt was shaking off his coat and barking, but the lizard was actually screaming. Kozmo had never heard a sound like it.

The lizard's accent was quite strange, now that she was talking. "What is it, what is it? Get them off me!"

"It's food!" Kozmo screeched at them from her hidden perch above. How did a lizard not like a delicious, leggy insect? Maybe it had to do with whatever the Yellow Six had done to her, Kozmo considered. Maybe they had erased Flicker's instincts? That was a horrifying thought.

But Kozmo couldn't help laughing, too. It really was quite funny to see them dancing around like that.

In the end, they bolted down the tunnel, leaving all the writhing delicacies behind, and Kozmo feasted on them herself.

She was just finishing up when she heard something in the distance. Kozmo snapped to attention. She could feel tiny vibrations in the walls. The fine hairs inside her sensitive ears twitched. Someone was coming.

Kozmo didn't know what to do. She didn't want to get

the intruder's attention, but she felt this strange desire to protect the other animals, too. She needed to know how far away the intruder was, at least—how much time she had. She let out one high screech, and the echo bounced back to her almost immediately. There was more than one. And they were close.

Runt and the lizard didn't even know they should run. Kozmo had to warn them! But if she showed herself now, she'd have to explain, and there wasn't time for that. If she could scare them into running, maybe they stood a chance to get away.

She hissed, and she screeched, and she flapped her wings.

Unfortunately, it worked too well. The dog and the lizard were terrified. Instead of running, Runt reacted how he always did in unfamiliar situations: he started yelling his head off.

The barks were ear-splittingly loud, and they got the attention of whatever was on its way.

Kozmo felt the vibrations quicken. Whatever was coming was headed right toward them!

30

Castor and Jazlyn were certainly far away from humans now. They were in one of the darkest tunnels, with no more vegetation, no man-made light source, and only their senses to guide them.

The tunnel smelled like stone walls and metal tracks and sulphurous river water leaching in, but underneath it all, Castor caught a note of *green*.

"The Greenplains are this way, I know it," he told Jazlyn.

The rabbit-panther had paused, though, a little less eager to bound down the path. For Jazlyn, fear lurked around every turn. "You can't only follow your nose, Castor," she warned. "There's something up ahead. Listen."

Castor's ears stood up. His body went rigid. "Runt?" he whispered.

Castor felt light-headed with a sudden surge of joy. His heart quickened in his chest. Before, when they'd first escaped, he had thought he was hallucinating. Now, there was no mistaking the sound of his brother's voice.

Or the distinct note of panic in it—something was wrong.

"RUNT!"

He didn't know exactly where his brother was, but instinct took over. Castor shot forward, and it was like his muscles belonged to someone else. Someone stronger. Faster. He bounded blindly, his legs churning with such speed that not even Jazlyn could keep up.

Through the mud, over the tracks, down into unknown darkness, Castor's eyes barely registered the turns and dips of the path. He was focused on something beyond this tunnel.

He saw his little brother, bounding after him down their alley in Lion's Head on too-big puppy feet. He saw Runt, breathless with excitement on their first hunt, zipping around Castor so fast he got tangled in his legs and tripped them both. He saw Runt hunting, and sleeping, and playing—always somewhere close behind Castor's shoulder. He saw the curiosity in those wide brown eyes as he asked Castor to tell him again about the latest news headlines and the Unnaturals reality show, and his dreams of the Greenplains. He saw Runt as he'd seen him in dreams during those long months in his cell at NuFormz: frozen in time on the dock in those moments just before the men had come and changed everything. Goofy and trusting and vulnerable and full of love for his big brother.

Then he saw him for real. Up ahead, silhouetted under the dim tunnel lights, was a shepherd dog. Thinner than Castor remembered and with mangier fur, but familiar all the same. More than familiar. That particular stance, that angle of the head, that flop of the left ear was *unmistakable.*

"Brother!" Castor barked an ecstatic greeting. He had lost so much. He couldn't believe Runt had come back to him.

"Castor?" Runt gasped. Then his teeth shone in the dopiest, most welcome grin Castor had ever seen.

"Broth—oof!"

Castor didn't know what hit him. The way it cracked

182

his skull, making the overhead lights turn into an explosion of stars, it could've been a Crusher Slusher. It felt like someone had thrown one of the weights he used to train with back at NuFormz at his head.

He felt an immediate surge of nausea, and Castor flopped to the side as he dry heaved, blinking fast and waiting for his vision to clear.

Then there was a *whoosh* of air as the thing circled back, and Castor ducked down, flinching for a second hit. But it wasn't coming for him this time. He saw a shock of orange, a flash of wing, and then Runt's wide eyes as whatever it was—some unidentifiable *creature*—latched its teeth onto the scruff of the young dog's neck and, lurching awkwardly with the dog's unfamiliar weight, carried him away.

No. Castor blinked at the empty tunnel. *No no no no no.*

He scrambled to his feet, swaying with dizziness after the blow. He tore after them, and soon Jazlyn was by his side again, recovered from her terror.

"My...brother..." He panted an explanation. "Have to...find..."

She gave a quick nod and shot forward, the dirt spraying up behind her. Jazlyn was impressively agile, weaving around pipes and bounding over gaps in the tracks, but the head injury hit Castor harder than he'd thought, and he struggled to keep up in the darkness.

I will not leave him, Castor vowed, squinting for a glimpse of those dark wings flapping ahead. When he couldn't see the wings any longer, he tried to focus on just the screeching, but it seemed to be bouncing all around the caves and echoing through the tunnels, so it was impossible to find his way.

I can't . . . lose him, Castor thought. *Not again.*

But try as he might, his muscles were starting to fail him now. His legs grew clumsy, and his talons snagged. Castor stumbled, then lurched, and finally collapsed, and he was left in darkness.

31

LEESA HAD SAID THEY NEEDED PROOF THAT OTHER PEOPLE were involved if they were going to help Pete, but being grounded, Marcus didn't exactly have much access to other people. He did have access to Bruce, though, and for the first time, Marcus was actually looking forward to spending some time with his stepdad.

That it was for the sole purpose of discovering incriminating information that would ensure Bruce was locked up forever was beside the point.

Marcus's parents were arguing a lot lately, and Bruce was spending a lot of late nights at work. Marcus took the opportunity of the building family tension to do some snooping. He snuck into Bruce's office and took a look around.

The walls were covered in boring sciencey stuff—biology illustrations and food-chain diagrams and charts of elements. Everything was pretty organized on the desk. There wasn't much in the drawers except an old tablet and a stack of notepads—Bruce was so ancient he actually still took notes. Like, with an actual pen.

Marcus heard the squeak of Bruce's tennis shoes and realized he had lost track of time. Just before Bruce opened the door, Marcus dove behind one of the white curtains covering the windows. A ton of dust bunnies crawled up his nose, and as Marcus held his breath to keep from sneezing, he heard Bruce giving a voice command on his handheld.

"Eris."

Bruce waited a beat while it connected. Then Marcus heard a volley of words on the other side, and listened to Bruce's frustrated inhales as he kept trying to cut in.

"I know," he kept repeating. "I know. I'm not backing out."

More sighing, and Marcus heard his fingers tapping—must be accessing the slipstream.

"I have the data right here, and I'm telling you we're not ready to move to H-trials yet. That timeline is impossible without more experiments." He sighed. "Fine. I said, fine! But it isn't right."

Bruce huffed and stormed out of the room, and Marcus scrambled out from behind the curtain.

Of course his notes would be on the slipstream—easily accessible from home or the office! Marcus had to get out of here, though. That was close, and if Bruce found him in his office, Marcus wouldn't just be grounded, he'd be strapped to his bed in a straitjacket.

When he got back to his room, Marcus took out the mess of cords and stream accessories from the box he'd shoved in the corner. He'd been locked out of the simulink before, but now that Marcus had a real purpose, he had a little more initiative and creativity. Using gaming codes from a defunct role-play set that connected players from all over the world, Marcus was finally able to get on to the slipstream. And after that, it didn't take him long to hack into Bruce's storage and access his files.

Pro tip: do not make SexySciFi your password. And definitely don't tape it under your tablet so you won't forget.

Also: don't be an idiot jerkwad.

Meaning: don't be Bruce.

That's how, under the guise of gaming in his room, Marcus managed to hack into Bruce's slipstream. He would take his time browsing all this highly confidential information on his floor-to-ceiling warp screen.

Unfortunately, the only thing on the data storage in the slipstream was a slideshow.

Marcus watched it eagerly, expecting images like the ones the mayor had shown of Pete: bad people doing bad things they would pay for.

Instead, Marcus saw images of his mom and Bruce's wedding, of tiny Pete holding tiny Marcus's hand, of Bruce looking nervous and scared but a lot more daring than Marcus could ever remember him looking since.

It almost made a tiny part of him feel for his stepdad. Almost.

But regardless of what Marcus thought of Bruce, he still hadn't fond any clues about the mayor's motives. Another dead end.

32

THE SCHOOL LEESA ATTENDED WAS IN A TIDY ONE-ROOM apartment in the Drain. After class Leesa lingered at her teacher's desk until the room had emptied out.

"How's everything going, Leesa?" Ms. Hoiles asked. Her teacher had short hair and a small nose that seemed to always be able to sniff out when something was bothering one of her students. "I saw your picture on the mayor's broadcast, and I wanted to commend you for what you did."

189

"I don't know if it turned out in the best way." The animals had been recaptured, and now Pete was in jail.

"Still," Ms. Hoiles said. "It takes a lot of guts to stand up for what you believe in. You're just like Fern in that book I gave you, eager to protect animals."

Leesa reddened. In all the commotion in the arena, she had managed to lose *Charlotte's Web*.

"I'm actually reading a new book now," she said, pulling out the Nancy Drew novel.

Ms. Hoiles reached for it and ran her hand along the old, cracked cover. "Why does this look familiar?" She opened the cover. "Oh! My goodness! Of course. It's the book I gave Francine Eris, though it was quite some time ago. However did you get it?"

Leesa looked away guiltily. "I, uh, borrowed it," she said with a shrug.

"I've been wondering how Francine was doing. Is she still very ill?" Ms. Hoiles's eyes crinkled with concern.

"I didn't know she was sick."

"Well, I guess that's good—she must be doing a lot better, then."

"What was wrong with her?" Leesa pressed.

"She had some very severe environmental allergies. Poor child was so sensitive to the sun, that the UV rays even affected her through the walls. By the time I was visiting her for private schooling, Francine was bed-bound."

"Well, she's definitely not anymore," Leesa said. She'd been in Francine's bed, after all.

"Perhaps she was sent to Paloma," Ms. Hoiles mused. "They have a lot more resources and vegetation, and I know the climate is much milder."

Leesa shifted in her desk, confused. *Paloma, the city to the south?*

"I thought no one from Lion's Head was allowed in there. After the great gate went up?"

Ms. Hoiles leaned against her podium. "Yes, last I heard Francine had been rejected for a mercy migration. Her family was pretty devastated, as they were running out of options. If you do see her, will you give her my best?"

"Sure," Leesa said. She felt bad deceiving Ms. Hoiles, who had always been kind to her, but this sounded like another clue, even if Leesa didn't quite understand how yet.

What was it that Mayor Eris had said about the world being complicated?

This was for the greater good.

33

LEESA'S PHONE DINGED ON HER WAY HOME FROM SCHOOL.

"Pls Lees, let's talk."

Not again.

Antonio had been sending dozens of texts begging her to meet with him so he could explain. Leesa had ignored every one, but for the first time, she reconsidered. Now she actually *wanted* someone to explain. Something. Anything. Her head hurt from trying to sort through it all.

Instead of texting back, she headed straight for his house. He and Vince lived in one of the train cars on the defunct green line. It was a slum, but it was home; even when Vince had gained power, they'd stayed in that same caboose cab. Leesa rapped hard on the metal of the car, and several of the neighbors peered out. The Drain wasn't much for privacy.

Antonio finally stumbled to the door, and his eyelids, which were half-closed from sleeping all morning, flew open when they saw her.

"Leesa!" He lunged forward to hug her, but Leesa put up her hand.

"First, why weren't you there?" she demanded.

"What?"

"Why. Weren't. You. There?" she repeated, practically yelling it the second time.

What she meant was, *Why did you betray me?* Tears sprang to her eyes.

Antonio's cheeks got all red, like he'd been slapped, and when he didn't answer, Leesa continued her assault. "Tell me about the mayor."

Tell me why I'm wrong. Tell me why there's hope. Tell me who to trust.

"She's different than we thought," Antonio said. He gripped her shoulders, his eyes bright. "It's the revolution,

Leesa. Finally. Us Drainos are finally going to rise into the light. She even put Vince in charge of the Kill Clan."

Leesa narrowed her eyes. "What the heck are you talking about? Does this have to do with the shot that Pete gave the Vicious?" Pete had said he thought it had to do with something bigger, right?

"You mean your friend's stupid brother? That vet tech in the news?" Antonio snickered. "That was, like, beta level. Vince says they're way past that now. Bruce is getting close."

"Close to what? And *Vince* is involved with Bruce's world?" Leesa really didn't like the sound of that. Antonio's brother was a gang leader who had his hands in just about every pot of illegal activity in the Drain.

"Look, I can't talk about it here." Antonio looked around at his neighbors. The makeshift houses were practically on top of one another, and lots of eyes had appeared through cracks and flapping plastic windows. "But I'll take you somewhere where I can prove it," he said into Leesa's ear, standing a little too close to her.

For one second, Leesa wanted to believe everything Antonio said, she wanted to believe that everything could go back to being easy. And then Antonio finished his thought.

"All you have to do . . . ," he whispered, a smile in his

voice, ". . . is be my girlfriend."

Leesa recoiled backward, almost stumbling off the platform onto the tracks.

"I already told you I don't like you like that," she snapped. "So, what? You think you can blackmail me into it?"

"Leesa—"

But Leesa had heard enough from Antonio. She turned and ran, blocking out the sound of his voice following her down the platform.

34

WHEN CASTOR CAME TO, HE SMELLED SOMETHING FOUL, and his nose wrinkled as he opened his eyes. That was even more unpleasant, since the first thing he saw was a furry white face with two glowing red eyes, inches from his own. Its whiskers were poking Castor in the snout— that's how close it was—and Castor caught a flash of a white fang.

"Ah!" He flinched instinctively, aware of his vulnerable position. But Castor wasn't going to die in an ambush, lying prone on the floor. An instant later, he was scrambling to his feet and barking wildly.

"Whoa!" Jazlyn skittered out of the way just before Castor sank his teeth in. "It's just me!"

"Sorry." Castor sighed, relaxing.

It took Jazlyn longer to recover. When he saw how his friend's usually sleek panther's coat was frazzled in alarm, Castor had to laugh.

"You're puffed up all the way down to the tip of your panther tail!" he snorted.

Then Castor remembered another puffed-up tail with its flash of orange disappearing down the tunnel with his brother, and his smile fell away. He sank back down, hanging his head.

"Here," Jazlyn said gently. "Have something to drink."

The suggestion seemed strange—other than a bit of mud seeping down from the walls, liquid was scarce underground—until he realized that the dull rushing sound in his ears that he'd attributed to the headache was actually running water. Looking around him, Castor was surprised not to recognize his surroundings at all.

They were on some type of a platform. Instead of the low beams of the tunnel, a space opened above them, and overhead, a mess of pipes fed liquid into a man-made stream. Castor followed it with his eyes and saw that the stream fell abruptly in a waterfall. He couldn't see where it ended, but the sound told him it was a long drop.

Castor stepped forward and leaned over the surging water. Except it wasn't actually water.

"Ugh!" He recoiled back, wrinkling his nose and gagging. It was the foulest thing he'd ever smelled, and that was saying a lot—Castor had been around *humans* for the last several months.

"Not there. *There*." Jazlyn nodded toward a curtain of liquid that gushed down from one of the pipes. "I don't know what the other ones are, but that one's water, at least."

Castor approached it warily, but once he felt the spray hit his nose, he was slurping away. He hadn't realized how parched he was until he felt its coolness running down his throat.

It reminded him of the moment he'd first met Jazlyn, when she'd offered him the water bottle in her cage at NuFormz. Back then, Castor had been all dog, and he'd been startled at the sight of the strange white rodent with long ears. He'd been wondering if she was food when she declared herself a friend instead. The thought was comforting, to think that she was still looking out for him, whatever else happened.

"Thank you," he said, taking a breath. Water dribbled down from his chin.

"I lost track of your brother," Jazlyn said, her voice heavy with guilt. "They flew up somewhere I couldn't follow. I found this place, though. When I went back for you, you were unconscious."

She must've dragged him all the way here. Castor couldn't imagine the strength and determination that it probably took, though he knew Jazlyn would be embarrassed if he mentioned it.

"How long have I been out?" he asked instead.

Jazlyn shrugged. "A little while."

Castor knew what that meant: *Long enough to lose any hope of catching the thing that took Runt.*

"I'll never see my brother again." The fact of it hit him low in the gut. It was hard to breathe.

"Well, that's not very optimistic."

"Jazlyn. We have no idea where we are, and these tunnels are a maze. Even if we knew where we were going, I can barely see in the dim light. I'm not fast enough to catch them, and you can't fly. How do you stay positive about something that's impossible?"

"Flying used to seem impossible to you, too, didn't it? So did winning a match."

Castor shook his head. This was different.

Jazlyn was insisting otherwise. "Remember training back at the Pit? Remember a certain bull-headed captain?"

"Moss." Who had given himself up so they could be free. How disappointed their captain would be to see how they'd failed.

"What did Moss tell us that very first week about working together?"

"That it didn't matter what team we were on, because everyone was doomed?" The zebra-bull had always been a little bleak. Castor was finally starting to appreciate his perspective.

Jazlyn twitched her nose dismissively. "You might not be nocturnal, but my night vision's pretty great. And I might've lost them around a turn, but you sure know how to track a scent."

"Your eyes, my nose." Castor considered.

"My legs, your wings," Jazlyn answered with a nod.

Castor wished they had Moss's strategy instead of just his advice to add to the mix, along with Enza's swordlike teeth and Samken's power—or even just their company—but it was a start, at least.

"It's still got a huge head start on us."

"And it's also carrying Runt's weight and will have to stop twice as often," Jazlyn pointed out.

"Okay then, Eyes, what did you see? What are we looking for?"

Jazlyn grinned. "I didn't get very close, but what I saw was a sort of . . . dog with wings. A bit like you, actually."

Another dog with wings. Castor cocked his head, unsure of what to make of that. Was this the result of his escape? Had the Whistlers created an Underdog 2.0 to track him down and teach him a lesson?

"What about you, Nose?" Jazlyn fired back.

Castor lifted his snout and sniffed the air. Even beneath the pungent odor of the stream, he could still catch a whiff of something else. There was trash, smog, asphalt, and a hint of peanut butter—the unique scent of Runt that he'd recognize anywhere—plus the awful antiseptic-coated-leather lab-animal smell of his kidnapper.

"I smell a trail," he answered. "Let's go!"

The search took longer than Castor wanted, but not nearly as long as he'd imagined. Castor often had the feeling that they were being watched, or that the walls were moving. Twice more they had close calls with humans, and when they finally caught up with the scent, it was in an abandoned train station dangerously near another platform village.

As soon as they entered the space, Castor's senses were sounding the alarm.

Humans, said the click of his talons on the tile floor.

Humans, said the signs written in humanspeak.

Humans, said the moving stairwell that climbed forever and never took you anyplace at all.

The place reeked of them.

There was also a faintly tropical smell in here, which Castor only recognized from the fried pineapple treats that the food carts used to sell at his matches.

It also smelled like Runt, which was really the only reason Castor kept going.

There was a little box with glass windows that said TICKETS, and perched atop was the creature. Runt was there, too, but the animal was mostly blocking him from view.

Castor looked at Jazlyn sidelong. She thought *this* looked like *him?*

This was no dog. The dogs he knew were black and tan, or gray, or white. He even knew a couple with spots, like the mean Dalmatian from the rival pack. He had never seen a dog with fur this color before, though. It was coarse, and long, and a deep reddish orange. Its tail was bushier than most, with a clean white tip.

And he wasn't sure you could call those things wings,

either. They didn't even have feathers—more like leather skin flaps, if you asked Castor. That was probably why it had let them catch up—its wings were too flimsy to carry any weight for more than a short distance.

It was a monster, though, that was clear. Castor hadn't realized there were other mutants than those he knew at NuFormz—those on Team Klaw and Team Scratch. Where had this one come from? Maybe it was one of the famed escapees Moss and Pookie had talked about, though that had seemed more myth than fact.

The creature didn't take flight. Instead, it stood right over Runt and looked Castor straight in the eye. Castor had been in enough street scuffles, and certainly enough official matches, to recognize a challenge when he saw it.

Back in the Dome, Castor had done whatever he could not to fight. Even when Laringo was coming toward him, Castor dodged, and pivoted, and flew away.

But this thing wasn't an Unnatural. And this wasn't entertainment. It had attacked his family.

Castor jerked his head around when he heard another animal's footsteps. He saw a giant lizard lumbering in, so loud that it seemed like it was trying to announce itself. Was this some sort of power play? Were they trying to surround him and Jazlyn? Were there more he should know about?

He had lost Runt once on the dock. Then he had watched as he was taken away, seconds before they were reunited. Whatever happened, Castor was not going to lose his brother again.

Castor bared his teeth. His jaws pulled back into a snarl, and he let out a growl that, echoing around the cavern, sounded more like a roar. Who would call him the Underdog now?

35

"SEE?" KOZMO WHISPERED TO THE COWERING DOG BEHIND her as the mutant dog took a wide, aggressive stance. "*Now* do you see?"

Runt had been claiming one of the mutants was his brother, the lost family member he'd been searching for, but that didn't matter much anymore. Whatever he had been before, this monster was not the kin Runt knew, Kozmo was sure of that. The serum made that impossible.

Things hadn't gone how Kozmo had planned, not at all. After all that time she'd spent watching Runt and the lizard, getting to know them so that they could be friends, Runt didn't even seem to like her.

She'd *saved* him, but Runt had wriggled so much in her grasp that she could barely fly with him, and when she finally set him down, instead of licking her face in appreciation like she'd seen him do to the lizard, all he'd done was moan that his best friend, the lizard, was gone. Well, she couldn't very well carry them both, could she?

A sunny smell entered the space, and Runt sat up. "Flicker?" he panted with relief.

She clomped into the subway station, her feet making sticky sounds on the floor, and when the new mutants locked eyes on the lizard, Kozmo knew her instincts had been right. These were aggressive mutants with a strong kill drive, and it was easy to see the murder in their eyes—*especially* the one that resembled Runt.

"Castor . . . ?" Runt said uncertainly.

The bird-dog narrowed his eyes and looked between Kozmo and Flicker, clearly deciding whose throat he should lunge for first.

Kozmo was ready. Though she had never fought before, she was pretty sure she knew what to do. Back in the room, the mutants had been in cages, under the control of the men, but she'd studied them from above for long enough that she understood their instincts. She had stood in front of Runt so that the mutants would register her as the primary target. Sure enough, when Kozmo jumped down, the mutants followed her in their pursuit.

"Get up there with Runt!" Kozmo shouted to Flicker.

But the lizard looked terrified and confused. Why wasn't she using her sticky feet to scamper up atop the ticket booth? It was probably that blue goo in the lab, burning off her footpads, Kozmo realized. The poor lizard was basically helpless. Kozmo swooped down and quickly yanked Flicker up by her tail, tossing her next to the dog, and they huddled together.

Kozmo wasn't prepared to take on two mutants, so to avoid the rabbit mix—clearly created when Bruce and the Yellow Six were testing bio versus machine flee-response compatibility—all she had to do was stay in the air. Easy enough.

Kozmo careened away and the dog snapped its wings open in pursuit. But with that sort of span length—at least ten feet—he needed space to gain speed. The low ceiling meant he could barely get in a few weak flaps before he had to cut back in the opposite direction.

His switchbacks were nothing to be proud of. The

eagle-dog didn't have the control Kozmo did. It was clear he had flown enough to understand how his wings worked—flap to go up, at least, and dip to come down—but they didn't seem *part* of him.

Runt had told her *allll* about his brother's career as a professional fighter on the way here, and while the so-called Underdog's feathers might've been a little prettier on a poster, Kozmo knew her scalloped gray wings were made for *survival.*

And if Bruce and the Six were here testing her, they'd give Kozmo a pass on all counts.

What did surprise her, though, was that the eagle-dog's movements weren't at all jerky. He didn't have that glazed look, either. Maybe after all this time, the lab was making progress with the newest serum?

The kill drive was definitely still there, though. The mutant dog was trying to herd her toward the lights to blind her, and it snapped its jaws at her as she dove down.

Kozmo darted, swooped, and cut across. She dodged the talon that was grasping for her, and instead turned her head to press her sharp teeth into the dog's furry ankle.

The mutant yipped in pain and jerked his fore-paw into his chest. The injury made his flapping more erratic, and he dropped back down to the scuffed marbled floor. He took one step and stumbled on the injured leg. Stupid.

"Leave him alone," Runt barked from atop the ticket booth.

Her new friend didn't understand what was at stake. He saw his brother, but Kozmo had learned not to trust appearances. You never knew what you might find below the surface.

Swooping down, this time, Kozmo went for the monster's neck. Her teeth went in, two needle points, and the mutant dog shook and wriggled. Kozmo felt a claw slice into her side—she'd forgotten about the vicious rabbit-panther—but still she held on tight.

"Stop it!" Runt cried. "No more!"

He threw himself off the ticket booth and onto their backs. The four animals slammed down to the hard floor, and their labored breaths echoed around the abandoned station.

36

Runt was an excellent hunter, and a great story-teller, but as the smallest omega dog of the pack, he'd always been weak. If Alpha had had his way, Runt would've been exiled along with their mother, but Castor had stood up for him then, and again and again growing up. He'd fought for Runt in spats over territory lines with other dogs, protected him from an entire rival pack on the dock across the city, and stood over him when the humans came.

Now, his little brother was the only animal that could save Castor from bleeding out at the paws of this monster, and Runt had stepped up, putting himself right in the middle of a fight—not just between two dogs, but between two mutants.

To Castor, that took more guts than anything he had done in the Dome.

He was proud. And for a second, he even thought that he, Jazlyn, and Runt could destroy the flying orange beast together.

But then Runt turned to face Castor and, blocking the creature, yipped, "Don't hurt her!"

"Me?" Castor snuffed in bafflement. "She had those little daggers hooked in *my* neck!"

Runt's hackles stayed raised in warning. He was afraid of Castor. His own brother! To Castor, this hurt more than the whole pack turning on him, more than Enza and Samken's recapture, more, even, than losing Pookie. Castor and Runt had known each other their whole lives. If Runt really believed he was a monster, could it be true?

"Runt, look at me," Castor whined. He put his belly on the ground and crawled forward, trying to look as nonthreatening as possible. "I'm your brother. A few feathers doesn't change that."

"Oh, I don't mind your wings," Runt said, perking up. Even now, Runt couldn't keep his tail from whipping. "They're amazing! They're better than the Invincible's tail, or the Mighty's horns! They were the best part of every match."

"You saw my matches?" Castor asked in wonder.

"Every one. Well, the highlights. The flash pictures only show little clips."

Castor was touched, but at the same time, the thought made him a little queasy. Runt had always been a fan of the Unnaturals gladiator reality show, but back then, he used to root for Laringo, the scorpion-tailed invincible tiger.

"I saw when you refused to fight. I saw when you learned to fly. I saw them say you were the winner."

Runt's voice was proud and full of awe, and Castor's heart swelled. During the hardest matches and his toughest times alone in his cell, he'd talked to Runt in his mind. Castor had wanted someone in the crowd rooting for him, as the human girl Leesa had for Pookie, and all those times he'd imagined Runt was in the stadium, cheering him on. And in a way, he actually was.

"Then what's wrong? Why are you shrinking away from me like that?"

Runt dipped his head down, and one of his ears flopped forward. "Kozmo says you're dangerous. That you'll hurt other animals, even though you don't mean to." His voice dropped to a whisper. "That you'll hurt my friends. My very *best* friends." He shot a look to the top of the ticket booth, where the lizard was lying on her belly and peering her head fearfully over the edge.

Oh, so the pineapple-smelling loud-foot was with him, not the creature. Figured—Runt was always picking up strays weaker than himself.

"I didn't know that was your friend," Castor started to explain, but Runt quickly cut in.

"That you'll hurt *me*."

That was what Castor had feared most. That he'd become cold. A killer. But he'd fought that with every ounce of his soul.

"I won't. Never. I'm still the same inside." Pookie had made him believe that, and it was the only thing that had saved Castor from crossing over. From becoming Laringo. "Don't you trust me?"

"Trust doesn't matter," the enemy mutant cut in. "Biology does. Did they give you the serum?"

"What?"

"The shot."

Castor thought back to that first day he'd spent in

the NuFormz lab. He remembered a needle the size of a rat's rib. The cold liquid shooting through his veins, stopping his heart for a few terrifying moments. And then the feathers poking up between his shoulder blades.

"We all got a shot," he pointed out. "It's what made us mutants."

"The mutant part isn't what matters," the creature said. "The kill drive is."

"Is that what made you try to drain my blood?" Castor snapped.

"I was protecting Runt," she said. "I don't have the kill drive. I'm not like them. Like you."

"Well, I don't have it, either," Castor insisted. "And neither do my friends. I don't know where you came from, but I sure never saw you in the NuFormz prison, or in the lab. Maybe we were given different shots."

The mutant paused and cocked her head, considering. "You don't have the jerky motions of the others I've seen. Or the flat voice. Or the dead eyes . . ."

Castor was relieved to hear her say that, while at the same time, a shiver went down his spine. Laringo was like liquid mercury on his feet, but otherwise, the lifeless gaze and weird voice described the Invincible exactly. Jazlyn shot Castor a look letting him know she was thinking it, too.

Castor could feel the other animal still watching him. She stared openly, rudely, like she was used to looking at things that couldn't see her. Her eyes were a deep, chocolate brown—smart, thoughtful. Her gaze made Castor uncomfortable, but it also made him feel warm somehow. If she wasn't trying to kill him, he could see how you might be drawn into her deception.

"Are you sure you only got one shot, and all it did was make you a mutant?"

"Yeah, that's *all*," Castor sniffed.

"The kill drive started showing up in Bruce's later serums, in a second test. It's like a virus, but instead of getting sick, you go mad."

Castor went quiet. He'd seen other diseases like that. Years ago, several dogs in his pack had been bitten by rabid raccoons and had gone mad. Was this like that? Was he going to start foaming at the mouth, and feeling his blood heat up, fueling his fury? Was he really going to turn into Laringo? A true monster?

Jazlyn didn't think so. She must've seen the fear in the whites of his eyes, because she stepped close to his side and raised her chin to the other mutant. Castor knew that took some real courage for the notoriously meek bunny, and he was grateful to his friend.

"You and Castor are a lot alike," Jazlyn pointed out.

"No, we're not!" Kozmo and Castor said in unison, scrunching up their noses in distaste.

The rabbit-panther loped around them in a circle, considering them from all angles. Castor didn't appreciate the scrutiny. He felt like Jazlyn didn't know him at all if she could lump him in the same category as this thing.

"You're both dogs," she said.

"That is not a dog, Jazlyn!" Castor protested.

"Well, canine, at least. And you both have wings."

"A bat is hardly like an eagle," Castor said. He ruffled his feathers and rolled his shoulders, extending his wings to their full span. He puffed his chest out proudly. "Eagles are majestic. Eagles are strong. Eagles are—"

"*Predators,*" Kozmo interrupted. "Don't they *hunt* bats?" Her beady eyes widened. "And hounds hunt foxes!"

A city dog, Castor didn't know much about foxes, but the fear on this one's face was pretty satisfying. Castor couldn't resist stirring it up a little more. "Maybe you should run, then," he growled.

But another growl bounced back to him in the cave, sounding much more like a roar. Castor felt the fur along his spine stand up, and he suddenly had the feeling that eyes were watching him in the darkness—pale, round tiger eyes with pupils no bigger than a speck.

"Maybe *you* should run," echoed a familiar voice.

Castor's blood ran cold. It was impossible. Castor had watched the light post tip over in the Dome. He'd heard the crunch. He'd seen the scorpion tail twitch from beneath the pole's weight and then lie still. Yet here his old rival was, back from the dead.

Truly invincible, despite all odds.

"Laringo."

37

Kozmo blinked in shock. Before her stood the most terrible thing she had ever seen. His body seemed as big as a train car. The powerful muscles of his shoulders rolled as he walked. His yellow teeth gleamed. His white-striped fur rippled. His segmented tail dangled its deadly stinger.

Behind him, nearly a dozen lesser mutants fanned out. Kozmo recognized some of these creatures from the white room—a hippo-headed wildebeest, a grinning horned hyena. All of them were fearsome, but none compared to the horrible creature at the helm.

The other animals seemed to recognize the scorpion-tiger.

"How did you survive?" Castor asked, clearly baffled. "We saw the pole fall on you! And what are you doing here? Did you change your mind? Do you want to join us?"

While Castor pelted the tiger mutant with questions, Runt cowered behind his brother, and Jazlyn was frozen in place and quivering all over. Kozmo didn't blame them.

But though her friends recognized the alpha animal, he most certainly did not recognize them. The tiger's eyes were glassy, vague, and rage filled. He didn't even seem to recognize the name they were calling him: Laringo.

This was the same scorpion-tiger Kozmo had seen Vince bring into the room—the one Bruce and the woman had talked about sending after her. But while it had seemed tame then, walking on a leash and lowering its head for the red-haired woman to pet it, now that she was seeing it up close and in kill drive, this mutant seemed like a man-made disaster. One part scorpion, one part tiger, one dark heart beating hatred with each breath.

"He's had the serum shot," Kozmo told them confidently. "He won't be . . . however you remember him."

"He wasn't much fun before," Castor admitted.

There was something about his eyes that was hypnotizing, that froze Kozmo right in place.

He wasn't looking at her, though. He was looking at . . . the wall? No, it was Flicker. The lizard had camouflaged herself so she was the exact shade of mottled gray-brown as the ceiling. She seemed to disappear and reappear so unexpectedly that Kozmo had forgotten she was with them. The scorpion-tiger had no trouble honing in on her, though. The lizard lifted her head and peered back at him with something like . . . tenderness.

"Master said not to hurt you," the tiger-scorpion purred.

Well, that's reassuring, Kozmo thought.

Apparently it didn't apply to everyone, though, because he turned away from Flicker, and the claws came out.

The hyena mutant leapt at her, and Kozmo ducked quickly. Then she sprang up just in time to miss a horn to the gut.

The tiger was stabbing his spiked tail down forcefully at the rabbit-panther, who had been jarred into action and was running circles around the snarling group.

There seemed to be a deadly mutant in all directions. They had to get out of this cramped space, or sooner or later someone was going to get unlucky.

Kozmo snapped her wings out, and almost crashed directly into the eagle-dog. He was soaring under the arch toward the escalators with Runt in his grasp, and then she glimpsed the swish of Jazlyn's long tail as she darted out toward the exit with the lizard on her back. That woke Kozmo up.

Just as the circle of dead-eyed villains started to close around her, Kozmo launched her body forward, slicing the air sideways with her wings and squeezing between them. She careened through the once-grand halls, letting out little hiccupy squeaks of terror despite her efforts to stay focused and brave.

Where were Runt and the others?

The hallways were dead ends, cul-de-sacs of boarded-up stores. A vision of the snake begging, *"Out! Let me outside!"* flashed in her memory, and Kozmo wondered if this advanced super mutant and his team were what the serpent had been trying to escape. Kozmo had to get back to the tunnels, at least, where in the twisting darkness she stood a chance at losing them.

Kozmo zoomed down toward the old subway platforms as Laringo and the other mutants pursued close behind. That she could fly was her one advantage, and as she sailed close to the slanting ceiling, the snarling beasts shoved onto the moving stairs all at once, forming a bottleneck.

Buying herself a few extra seconds, Kozmo dove under the plastic arm of one of the rusted-out ticket scanners. The hyena let out a high laugh that made her heart race. She fled toward the old platform, then used her hind fox feet to spring up, flinging herself onto the rusted tracks.

She flew through the tunnel, but the ceiling was low and her pursuers were tall. If they caught her, the leader could bat her out of the air with a swipe of his paw. It felt like only a moment before they were gaining on her again. Laringo trailed farthest behind; there was no urgency to the tiger-scorpion's movements, and that was even scarier. He took his time, stalking her with his slinking gate, as if he would catch her eventually, no matter how long she was able to stall.

At the next fork, Kozmo veered right, and her breath caught as something grabbed her and snatched her off the path—something scaly. Curling around her middle, the lizard's tail yanked her into a divot hidden in the darkest shadow of the track.

Kozmo could hardly see, but she could feel the other

animals around her—the giant lizard, Runt and his brother, the rabbit-panther—the warmth of their fur, their hot breath crowding close. After spending most of her life away from others, their touch made her feel nervous and safe at once.

"What are we going to do?" someone whispered.

"Can't we just stay here?" another, higher voice that sounded like Jazlyn's suggested.

"They've got our scent. Even if they pass us, it's only a matter of time before they loop back." That was Castor, pessimistic as ever.

"Maybe they'll give up," Kozmo said.

"The Invincible never gives up. That's why he keeps winning." That was Runt.

"So what do we do when they get here?"

"I've fought Laringo before." Of course, that was the eagle-dog again, bragging like a fool.

"So now you want to fight ten of them?" Kozmo challenged.

"You have a better idea?" Castor grumbled.

She did, actually. When she'd flown in with Runt, they'd crossed a sort of underground river that flowed into a wide pipe.

"Follow me," Kozmo said, and to her surprise, they actually did. Peering around for any sign of Laringo and his pack, she crept out of the hiding place and stealthily led the others through the darkness.

"That's a sewage pipe," Castor said when they got there, wrinkling his nose.

These NuFormz mutants were extremely delicate, weren't they?

"It's a way out of this," Kozmo said bluntly.

"Yeah, we might lose them for a minute, but Jazlyn and I saw where the pipes empty out."

"There's a long drop into a waterfall," Jazlyn explained, her voice grave. "We couldn't even see where it ended."

"So?"

"So, I don't want to drown!" Castor huffed. "And I don't want to hit whatever's at the bottom, either."

Not for the first time, Kozmo thought that this eagle-dog wasn't very bright. "You won't even hit the water. You have wings. When the water drops, you *fly*."

"Runt can't fly. Jazlyn and Flicker can't fly."

Kozmo had to stop herself from rolling her eyes.

"So when you fly, grab someone."

Jazlyn gulped and shrank down. She looked queasy at the thought.

"Those mutants aren't just going to jump into the pipe after us."

"They'll jump after me, though," Flicker said, slithering up beside them. "It's me they want."

Although Kozmo had heard the lizard's voice during her spying, it was the first time the lizard had spoken in front of anyone but Runt, and she saw the other animals start at the strangeness of her accent.

They seemed reluctant to trust her suddenly—especially given this new information that she was the one the mutants were hunting—but silhouettes began to appear down the tunnel, their jerky forms falling into a line as they got closer, and soon there wasn't a choice.

Kozmo waited until the last possible second to yell, "Now!"

She leapt into the filthy water first, the current taking her too quickly to turn around, and soon she was in the utter darkness of the pipe. Her stomach dropped as it took a sharp turn down, and she gasped for air as, again and again, the waves splashed over her head. She couldn't see where she was going or who was behind her until, suddenly, there was a faint circle of light, and she was airborne.

Hearing Jazlyn scream, Kozmo darted down and grabbed the long-eared cat by the scruff of her neck. Seconds later, Castor had snatched Runt, and they were all floating just above the spray of the falls.

Then, sure enough, the pipe spit the zombie mutants out, and one by one, they fell. When at last Laringo's broad, white head bobbed to the end, the tiger mutant let out a yowl and gripped the lip of the pipe with all of his claws. His body blocked the dam for a few futile seconds, but the water found its way around him, seeping through the cracks as the pressure built. Finally, there was a rushing sound, and Laringo burst forward into space, with no one to catch him. They watched the most terrifying mutant fall, end over end, stinger over maw, to whatever awaited him, all the way down.

"It worked," Castor breathed, his eyes bugging as he looked down after Laringo.

"Of course it did," Kozmo said, though she hadn't been so sure until the very last second.

38

Other than his secret sleuthing, Marcus didn't have a lot going on these days. He was thrashing around his room listening to Doomspeak when his door clicked open an inch.

"Marcus . . ."

"Mom!" He jumped to slam it closed. He might be grounded, but they had agreed that this was his personal space. If he wanted to jump on his bed like a five-year-old and sing at the top of his lungs, he didn't want to worry that someone was just going to barge in and laugh at him.

"I got sick of knocking." Her voice was annoyed. Though there were many times in the past that his mom had said she preferred to have him home, since he'd been grounded and the city was on lockdown, he knew that they'd both gotten on each other's nerves. "I said your friend is here."

Friend?

Marcus clicked off his inner-ear speakers and yanked the door open the rest of the way. Next to his mom was a girl with tanned skin, a blue streak of hair, and an uncomfortable expression.

"Leesa." Marcus blinked in surprise. They'd been in touch pretty much every hour since the visit to the prison, but Marcus hadn't expected her to visit him all the way from the Drain.

"Hey." She gave a little wave, fanning her fingers.

There was a beat while they all just stared at one another. Marcus felt intensely aware of how gross his shaggy hair must look from all the headbanging, and he realized he'd been sweating. Did his pits stink? Could she smell them? He tried to inhale deeply to check, but he knew he must look weird dipping his nose down like that, so he stopped. Now he was standing weirdly straight, wasn't he? He slouched his shoulders down, but that felt forced. Jeez, he was such a weirdo.

"Marcus?" his mom said. She was totally smirking.

Leesa looked past him expectantly. "Can I come in?"

"Uh, yeah. . . ." Marcus had never had a girl in his house before. Actually, he'd never had *any* friend over before.

Marcus glanced at his mom sidelong for permission. These days, she was spending most of her time worrying about Pete, so she'd gotten pretty lax about his grounding. Still, he was shocked she'd let Leesa through the front door. As a rule, his mom distrusted people from the Drain, and this was the girl he'd gotten into so much trouble with.

His mom crossed her arms. "Is your room clean?"

"Of course."

That was definitely not normal, and her forehead creased as she considered. Then she let out a big sigh. "Just don't tell Bruce, okay?"

She'd started to say that a lot lately. Bruce had been spending more and more time away from the house, and when he came home he looked haggard and acted even more irritable than usual. Marcus was totally fine with hardly seeing Bruce, but he could see the stress lines on his mom's face starting to deepen. Sometimes they fought about Pete, and sometimes he heard her crying in the bathroom—it was part of why he played his music so loud. It also helped to muffle his own worries, which seemed to get louder every day.

"I can't believe you actually have your own room," Leesa said, walking in.

Marcus shut the door behind her.

Leesa was craning her head around, taking every- thing in. He saw her looking at the warp screen that took up one whole wall. She took in his sound-blast system, his game vest, his cloud bed.

"You have got to be kidding me," she said, her mouth hanging open.

Marcus couldn't tell if it was in awe or disgust.

At the Skypark, the boys all bragged about the new tech. There were plenty of times that Marcus had wished he had the newest warp throne, or some stupid simu- link upgrade. For the first time, Marcus felt embarrassed about all he had instead of all he didn't.

"My parents like to buy me stuff so they can avoid actually talking to me," Marcus joked with an awkward laugh.

"I don't get to talk to my mom much, either," Leesa said.

There was a tinny barking sound, and Marcus's

automapooch almost rolled over Leesa's foot.

"What's that?"

"Zippy. They got him for me after I freaked out about the Underdog. Like it was going to just make me forget about the Unnaturals." Marcus rolled his eyes. "I programmed him to clean so I don't have to." He grinned conspiratorially, but Leesa didn't look impressed.

"Cool, so you freed mutant animals just to make a robot animal your slave?"

Marcus faltered, but when he looked at her, Leesa's mouth formed the tiniest smile. She was teasing him. She bent down and let the robot's nose sensors imprint her scent. It licked her hand, and Leesa grinned.

"Sorry to show up like this. It just seemed easier than trying to, like, pass secret messages through Joni or something. I figured the worst your parents could do was send me away. Where's Mr. Friendly, anyway?"

"Who, Bruce? Job hunting, supposedly." Based on the conversation he had heard, Marcus doubted that was true. "I broke into his office, but didn't find anything." Marcus didn't mention the family photos.

"He's probably with Vince." Leesa's mouth twisted. "Bruce and Vince are working together on something. What do you think that means?"

"I'm not sure. Did Antonio say anything else?"

Marcus asked, trying not to let his voice betray his jealousy. He couldn't believe Leesa was talking to that loser again after what he'd done.

"No." Leesa plopped onto his cloud bed with a huff. She shrugged. "He wouldn't tell me anything unless I agreed to be his girlfriend."

The moment seemed to stretch on forever, with just the sound of Zippy rooting around in his laundry. Marcus felt his face grow hot.

"And you . . . didn't?"

"No! Obviously."

Marcus felt more relieved about that than he wanted to admit. Leesa must've caught him grinning, because she was glaring at him now, her own cheeks red.

"What about you? Did you hear anything else from Pete?"

"Oh," Marcus's face fell. "Joni didn't tell you?"

Leesa shook her head. "Tell me what?"

"He's not at the jail anymore. My mom went to see him, and they just said he'd been transferred to a more secure facility, but they won't tell us where." Just thinking about it made him feel sick all over again.

Leesa blinked. "How is that legal? He didn't even DO anything! Where do you think they took him?"

Marcus shrugged. It was pretty much all he thought

about, and all his parents argued about. "Bruce claims he's at the Greenplains, and that they have him helping with the mutant transitions or something, but who knows? Bruce isn't exactly trustworthy. Anyway, they have the island and the Greenplains totally blocked off, so what? We just never see him again? They keep pushing back the so-called trial." Marcus shook his head bitterly. "We never should've freed Team Scratch."

"Marcus, don't say that." Leesa's face was firm.

Marcus thought of Pookie and all Leesa had lost, and he felt guilty for wishing they'd done nothing, but now that some of the animals were back in custody and his brother had disappeared, it just felt like their big escape was basically all for nothing.

"You should probably go," he told Leesa. He was afraid he was going to start crying in front of her, which was about the only thing that could make her feel worse right now.

"No. Stop it."

Despite her hard words, Leesa was scooting closer to him on the bed, and she leaned into him. They sat like that for a couple of minutes, shoulder to shoulder. Marcus could feel the warmth of her forearm through the mesh sleeve of her shirt. Her wrist bones seemed super tiny to him, and he noticed that her black nail polish was chipped, which for some reason he really liked. He did actually start to feel a little better and thought he could stay still like that for an hour or two, or maybe a month, until his life got a little easier, but as always, Leesa was on to the next plan.

"We need to discredit the case against him. All they really have is that video footage."

Marcus perked up, brainstorming. "And Pete said the mayor and Bruce were there making him do it. Maybe we can find the rest of the footage and get a clearer picture of what went on. I'm an ace hacker," he bragged. "If I could cut into the government-monitored slipstream . . ."

Leesa pursed her lips, unconvinced.

"Or, we could actually break into the facility and find the shots Pete said were in Bruce's lab. And if we don't find them, at least we'll know what's really going on with the animals there."

Marcus shook his head. "I love how you think sneaking out, going across the city, breaking into a facility that's on an island, and under investigation, AND controlled by the mayor is going to somehow be easier than a few shortcuts on the slipstream."

She looked at him sidelong, but Marcus was beaming. He really did love that about her.

"Well, both your brother and stepdad do work there,"

Leesa said wryly. "We should be able to walk right in."

Marcus snapped his fingers suddenly. "Pete's air-car! Still has all the clearance stickers. And a spot in the NuFormz hub. If I could just figure out what I did with Pete's keys after we took them the day of the escape."

The automapooch was smashing against the leg of the bed trying to get under it, making all these crazy beeping sounds along with the fake barks.

"Zippy, leave it," Marcus commanded, but it had something in its plastic teeth that it was trying to pull free.

Leesa reached for it, and she pulled out the tangled mess of keys. Of course, a single, filthy sock—Unnaturals brand, which he still wore only because he had like thirty pairs of them from his fan days—was caught on the metal.

At least it wasn't underwear, Marcus thought, his face flushing.

Leesa jangled the keys in front of his face. "Let's fire this baby up and go find our next clue!"

39

"Now what?" Kozmo asked.

The group was sprawled out on the ground next to the toxic falls, drying off. Castor had watched the winged fox joke with his brother, and he saw Runt's goofy, over-the-top laugh in response. He noticed how Jazlyn didn't shrink around Kozmo anymore, either. Her shoulders were relaxed, her chin high, and she seemed downright chatty, which was unusual for the soft-spoken mutant rabbit.

Not as chatty as the lizard, though. Flicker had been oddly silent throughout their initial meeting, but now she and Runt were talking excitedly about the escape, and her high, nasally voice made his ears hurt. It sounded like . . . humanspeak.

"Why do you talk like that?" Castor barked sharply. All three heads snapped toward him, startled, but he held the lizard's gaze.

"I, um . . . grew up with humans." Flicker shifted closer to Runt.

"She lived with them her whole life," the dog yipped, already defensive about this new friend of his.

"That's why I wanted to leave," the lizard explained in her weird accent. "I was tired of being poked and prodded every day."

Jazlyn looked at Castor with sympathetic eyes. They could both relate to that.

But though Castor trusted Jazlyn's instincts, he just couldn't bring himself to trust these new animals like she did. He had been most worried about the fox-bat, but now it was Flicker who made him most suspicious.

"I think we should go our separate ways," Castor told the lizard. "Laringo will follow you anywhere, didn't you say that? Well, we can't afford to get caught by the humans. I'm not going to lose my family again."

"Castor, the humans are following *all* of us," Jazlyn reasoned. "And you should know better than anyone that we're all orphans now, and all family." Her red eyes had a fiery intensity to them, and Castor remembered how she'd stuck by him again and again, while his own pack had turned their backs on him.

"I just want to make sure we get to the Greenplains," he told Jazlyn. "Isn't that the most important thing?"

"But Flicker can take us there!" Runt brightened up. "She knows the tunnels, and the river, and the shortcuts to the trains, and everything outside, too."

"Is that true?" Castor asked the lizard. "You know how to get to the Greenplains?"

"Yes . . ." The lizard's eyeballs darted.

"Isn't that the most exciting news EVER?" Runt cut in. Runt bounded around the tunnel, and before he knew it, Castor's own tail was wagging, too.

"All right, then," he said, barking a laugh. "I guess we're all going to paradise."

40

Kozmo was a survivalist, and usually, she preferred the predictable. Back in the room, she'd counted the mutants at night, so that she'd have a better idea of when Vince would set up fights and when Horace would arrive with new creatures and when Bruce would be back. She had noted which sleeping animals attracted which bugs, so that she'd always know where to look for food when she needed it. She had memorized exactly when the lights turned on each morning so that she could avoid any unnecessary contact with humans, and when they clicked off each night, so that she could hunt and collect materials for her nest. Kozmo's days were a controlled experiment; she always liked when her hypothesis of how each would go was correct.

Outside of the room, though, her life was the opposite of routine, or predictable. Though she could see in the dark, Kozmo might as well have been walking through these tunnels blind, since she had no idea what might lie around each turn. The variables were infinite, and her days were all trial and error. And oddly, she loved it!

She loved the uncertainty. She loved the newness. She loved how unlike everything she'd ever known it was. It wasn't about the actual places—the pipes and tunnels—it was about the discovery of what might come next. It was about the Greenplains, held in front of her like bait.

It helped that there was someone else to worry about a few of the variables now, someone to help when she got stuck. It didn't matter whether Kozmo knew what was around every corner. Though Flicker wasn't a great hunter, or fighter, or climber, she sure had a great sense of direction.

Castor was skeptical, of course. You couldn't please that eagle-dog. He kept asking, "Is this north? Are we under the river? We've gone five hundred paw ticks, is that too far? Aren't the Greenplains west?"

But Flicker seemed to anticipate every twist and turn in the underground labyrinth, avoiding the subway lines populated by humans, instead guiding them to hidden passages and through trapdoors. At the end of that first day, Flicker wrapped her sticky digits around a lever and when she pulled the door open with a creak, all any of them could see at first was *sunlight*.

The sight of something so beautiful finally shut Castor up.

They were *outside*. Not just outside—in another *world*. Until now, Kozmo had only known the room with its man-made walls, its white paint, its greenish light. And then the tunnels with their dark muskiness that hung in the back of her throat. This was a full-on assault of the senses.

Kozmo wiggled her paws into the sand, and it was hot, and soft, and yellow, and grainy, and almost overwhelming. She let the sunlight hit her full in the face and it made her eyes water and her nose sneeze and her mouth smile so, so big. Even though she could see better in darkness and the daylight made her a bit sleepy, the warmth on her back felt fantastic. There were no walls, no zombie animals, no humans. Whatever happened next, Kozmo knew she was going to be okay.

Castor and Runt were running around excitedly, wagging their tails and wrestling in the sand, and Jazlyn had raced out a mile and back lickety-split to test her legs. Kozmo would have figured that the lizard would be sunning its scales, but she noticed its eyes were clicking around nervously. Like it was actually afraid to be outside. Or maybe it was just afraid of Castor.

"This isn't the Greenplains," the eagle-dog said, squinting into the pale horizon. "I thought it was just across the river?"

"We had to take the long way if you didn't want to get captured. Paradise is up ahead," Flicker answered, and plodded on.

They encountered obstacles, of course—many every day—but each one seemed an adventure on the road to the great Greenplains. The desert was a hard place, but Kozmo found that having friends nearby meant that she could hold her fear at more of a distance.

They had lots of time to talk. She told them about Vince and the Six, but her life had been small and contained, and quite lonely, which she worried didn't make for good stories, so mostly Kozmo listened and began to notice things about her companions. Watching the other mutants in the room from a distance for so long had made her a top-notch noticer.

When she learned that Jazlyn had grown up in labs, like Kozmo had, she noticed that, as fast as Jazlyn was, when she ran, she favored the outsides of her feet. The wires of a cage had probably made her footpads tender. Kozmo had seen that happen in the Room.

She noticed that, even though Castor thought he was the one protecting his little brother, whenever there was a hint of a threat, it was Runt who trotted ahead. He pretended he was just chasing some bug or playing a game, but Kozmo saw the way the fur rose on his haunches as he cut between Castor and whatever worried him.

She noticed that Flicker still seemed nervous around mutants, but played nonstop with Runt, tossing tumbleweeds for him to fetch and tackling the dog on the dunes. And when she was fearful, the friends made each task into a small adventure, chattering to each other excitedly.

Kozmo wanted to join in sometimes, but it was hard to be a third friend with best friends.

That was okay, though, because in the desert, there were other things she could concentrate on. Like trying to survive.

Jazlyn went on scouting missions, racing ahead of the group to see what was over the next dune. Then she showed them how to suck water from cactus fruit, which she'd learned as a science class pet, and Kozmo and Castor took turns flying and surveying for food, which was scarce. And once Flicker got more comfortable in the sun, she began to sing songs to pass the time. For a lizard, she really had a wonderful voice.

When they'd gone two days without anything to eat, Kozmo had a strange instinct take hold of her, like a distant memory. Hearing a little scratching sound, her large ears swiveled toward it and she stared hard at the ground.

"What now?" Castor asked impatiently.

"Let me try something," she murmured, and though she was pretty sure this move was meant to be done in the snow—the land of her ancestors on one side—she tried it, anyway.

Pushing off hard with her back legs to spring high into the air, she leapt up, she whipped down, she dove deep, and then she started digging furiously.

Jackpot!

When Kozmo burst out of the sand with her paws and mouth stuffed with scorpions, it caused quite a commotion of howls, barks, growls, and hisses.

"Look at their stingers!" Castor yapped. "They're just like Laringo's. She's trying to kill us!"

"What are you talking about?" Kozmo laughed,

almost choking on her mouthful of food. "They're not Laringos. They're food. And they're *delicious!*" She crunched a couple more tails between her teeth and gulped them down before holding out a pawful to the bird-dog.

"Interesting," he said as he chewed. Even Castor had to admit that there was a certain satisfaction in eating something that resembled his nemesis.

It was Runt who had the best nose for water, though.

"Water!" he barked sharply one afternoon, and just the word was enough to make Kozmo's tongue spasm with want. "I smell it." His tail stiffened into a straight line behind him. "And I *seeee* it! Awooooooooo!" He howled, taking off to the west.

"Wait!" Flicker exclaimed. The urgency in her voice was alarming, and all the animals went on high alert.

Kozmo tore off after Runt.

Jazlyn's super-charged panther legs beat them both there, though, and before they reached the edge of the desert, the land had started to get swampy. When they caught up to their friend, Jazlyn was stuck right where she stood.

"Quicksand," Flicker explained.

"I saw the water, though," Runt insisted. "A lake. A river . . ."

"A mirage," the lizard said. "It wasn't real."

"Guys, we've got to hurry! Help her. It's okay, Jaz, we've got you," Castor said. One thing Kozmo did notice was that Castor was a pretty good friend.

By then it looked like Jazlyn's legs had been shortened by half. She was sinking right into the gritty muck. They had to form a chain and use one another's strength to pull her out. Kozmo thought that holding paws with everyone all in a line was probably the most exciting thing that had ever happened to her, and when they finally pulled Jazlyn free, the success rejuvenated the group.

Still, each day walking felt longer than the last. There was only the sand, and the sky, and the unforgiving sun. The sand was scalding, and the tiny grains reflected the light, blinding them sometimes and tricking them others. The sky, which had once seemed so open, now felt oppressive. The animals had escaped the humans and evaded the zombie mutants, but there was no outrunning the sun. For Kozmo, a night creature, it felt like being cooked alive. Flicker, with her scaly skin, seemed to be doing surprisingly well.

Runt stayed upbeat. He bounded along beside Flicker, his tongue dripping as he panted from the heat.

"We're almost there!" Runt insisted every few miles.

"The Greenplains, can you believe it? It's gotta be just over that hill, right? It's gotta be. Right, Flicker? Right?"

"I'm so glad we're friends!" Flicker beamed, but she was looking a little dehydrated now. It seemed that beyond each dune, there was only more sand.

From the air, the landscape looked even more desolate to Kozmo, and she found that flapping her wings was a dangerous waste of energy. Now, the animals walked in a sagging line, and their pace had slowed to a crawl.

At night, it got so cold that they all snuggled together in a heap. Kozmo was still not used to being touched by other creatures, but she found that when she nuzzled against Jazlyn's fuzzy bunny coat and Runt rested his head on her bushy tail, it was actually kind of nice.

41

You're in the nest, snuggling against your litter-mates. You can't see any of them, but you're drawn to the warmth, and the soft fur, and the gentle sounds of breathing.

One by one, the bodies disappear around you, until you are alone. It is so quiet now. You are so cold.

A man's voice. "I can make more. All I need is a dish and some cells. We're all just clusters of cells, right?"

You don't know where you are, and you can't find out unless you screech, and you can't screech or you'll be discovered.

You lie shaking in the dish for a long time, not knowing what to do.

Then footsteps come. Two feet and an upright form. You think it is the man, but it doesn't smell like chemicals like he does. It smells like fur. Like home.

The orangutan picks you up from the lab dish and hides you inside its long, orange fur, and walks away.

Who knew it was so easy to just walk away?

For weeks, until you are big and strong, you live on its milk. You also live on its love.

You'll forget this creature because you are so small and so young, but somewhere inside of you, the lesson is still there: you can't do everything on your own.

42

WHEN CASTOR AWOKE, HE THOUGHT OF HOW NICE IT WAS to be snuggled up with friends in the warm sand instead of lying on the cold, hard floor of a cell all by himself. It reminded him of being a puppy in the middle of the dog pile. He yawned and stretched a paw over his brother, and felt scales. And something like a coiled rope. And then he heard a percussive sound, a familiar sound—a sort of *sssss*.

Castor's eyes snapped open.

There were Runt, and Flicker, and Jazlyn, and Kozmo, all sleeping soundly.

But between their bodies, a dozen serpentine bodies were coiled up. Sometime in the night, the dog pile had become a snake pit. Apparently in the cold desert night, Castor wasn't the only one who wanted something warm to cuddle up against.

Why'd it have to be snakes? Castor thought.

He knew he should leap up. He should warn his friends. He could fly away in seconds. He could catch the snakes unaware.

But it didn't much matter what his brain was saying; his body was rooted to the spot. Though he was in one of the driest places possible—a desert—Castor felt like he was underwater. Though the rising sun was already making the ground hot, he felt his blood run cold. And though these were ordinary snakes and he was a mutant who'd been trained as an elite fighter, the scales and tails all blurred together, and Castor only saw one thing when he looked at them: Deja.

Castor shuddered as he heard the *sssss* that still haunted his dreams.

The desert fell away, and he was transported back to the Dome, to his match against Deja.

"S-s-stupid," Castor heard Deja scold, as he felt her

fangs sink into his tender nose.

"Trust is for s-s-suckers, s-s-shepherd dog," she'd told him as she coiled around his stomach and started to squeeze.

"S-s-sorry." He saw her unhinged smile just before she bit his ankle.

"Stay still," he heard the human, Pete, say later, as he was stitching Castor up.

Sssss

Sssss

Sssssssssssssssssssssssssssssssssssssssssssssssss

"Castor? Castor! Castor, RUN!"

Vaguely, Castor thought he heard his name. But the rattling was louder now, all around him. It was all he could focus on.

"What's wrong with him? Why isn't he moving? Brother, help! More are coming!"

"I think he's in shock. At NuFormz, there was a butterfly-snake. On the opposing team. He fought her once and—"

"The Cunning. They broadcasted the match on buildings all over Lion's Head. We watched from the alley."

"She escaped—I saw her. She was looking for a way home, a way to the desert. Maybe this is her kin."

"I can't hold them off much longer. Somebody do something! CASTOR!"

43

CASTOR WAS IN PAIN—THAT'S WHAT REGISTERED FIRST. HIS tail. No, his face. No, his belly. He was fairly uncomfortable all over.

"What's happening?" he howled, though in the next instant, the world snapped back into focus, and the scene became clear.

Castor was traveling at breakneck speed over yellow dunes. His soft belly was being scratched by sand, cacti, tumbleweeds, and anything else that got in his way. His head bobbed wildly, his nose smashing into the ground with each twist and turn. And his tail—what was pulling it so hard?

Castor twisted his shoulders around, and craned his neck to see that Kozmo, that sneaky fox-bat, was gripping the tip of his tail in her mouth. As she flapped her sinister gray wings overhead, she was *dragging him* along behind her.

Kozmo was chanting something, but at first Castor couldn't understand her because his fluffy tail was muffling her words. She shifted the tail in her mouth, catching the sensitive middle part of it with one of her pointy little teeth.

"Ow!" Castor yipped.

"Sorry," she said automatically.

But now that Kozmo could talk clearly, the next thing she said was a lot less polite.

"Come on, serpent friends!" she barked loudly. "He's the one you want."

Serpents?

Suddenly Castor remembered the situation he was in. The desert. The nest of rattlesnakes. Feeling paralyzed at the thought of fighting them. Then he'd blacked out.

Oh, no. Were Jazlyn and Runt okay? Did they need him?

He twisted back around. He couldn't see his pack, but he did see a whole line of snakes making soft *S*'s in the sand, zigzagging after them.

There were even more than before!

"The eagle-dog is an enemy of your family!" Kozmo bellowed. "This guy hurt Deja!"

What?!

"I did not!" Castor growled. "If anything, she hurt me!"

The snake family didn't seem to care, though. They were wriggling toward him with fangs bared and rattling tails held high. The percussive sound wormed its way into his ears. Castor felt dizzy.

To make matters worse, Kozmo seemed to be slowing down.

"Come and get him!"

He'd known from the beginning he couldn't trust her, but he'd never imagined she could be this heartless. She'd seemed to really care for Runt. Apparently, that had all been an act. Or maybe this was all one big plan to take his place. Did she think she could let the snakes kill him and then run back to his brother and best friend and try to buddy up? Did she think they wouldn't see right through her scheming? Did she think they wouldn't mourn him?

Well, she'd underestimated Castor, at any rate. He'd been a scrappy warrior in territory brawls in the alleys of Lion's Head. He'd taken on an entire enemy pack once to protect Runt. He'd gone head-to-head with the deadly, invincible Laringo, and he'd helped his team escape their cruel human captors. Castor might be an underdog once again, but he was not going down without a fight.

In his head, Castor started to strategize. What would his old mentor, Pookie, say about taking on twenty snakes on their home front? Castor was a fast runner and a smart fighter. He had the advantage of sharp talons and powerful wings.

But that was only if he could use them. He couldn't do anything with Kozmo holding him by his tail.

"Let me go!" Castor growled, thrashing in her grip. "What, leading the snakes to me isn't enough? I knew you were sneaky, but I didn't think you were such a coward. At least give me a chance to fight them on my own!"

But instead of releasing him, Kozmo started to pull on his tail again. Now he felt her back paws wrap around his tail, gripping it like a rope. She was dragging him again, this time into something . . . wet? Though he couldn't see behind him, Castor felt something sticky on his hind legs. It only lasted a moment, though. Soon he wasn't touching the sand at all as, grunting, Kozmo began to lift him up.

The snakes were nearly upon them now. She was dangling him in front of their eyes like a cat dangles a mouse—playing with it, taunting it. She might as well hand him over on a silver platter!

Castor's eyes widened. His heart pounded. His whole body started to shake. He imagined all those fangs sinking into him at once, all those scales constricting around him and cutting off his breath. It was a bad way to go. . . .

As the snakes surged forward, Castor let out one last bark of defiance, and Kozmo yanked him upward suddenly.

Below them, the snakes had not only stopped slithering . . . They'd started to sink.

The quicksand!

Bit by bit, the earth opened to swallow the serpents up. And even as Kozmo struggled to hold Castor's weight, she didn't dare lower him down until the last snake was out of sight. When, with a belch, the sand closed up once again without so much as a ripple, she finally set him gently on the firm desert floor a safe distance away.

By the time Castor's heart rate had slowed enough that he could speak, Jazlyn had arrived with Flicker riding on her back and Runt panting by her side.

"I can't believe it worked!" Runt cheered, licking Castor's face excitedly.

Jazlyn bowled into him, wrapping her strong panther paws around him in an embrace that knocked Flicker off her back and Castor to the ground. After a second, she stood up, embarrassed, and dusted herself off. Though Jazlyn was smiling, her red eyes were still clouded with worry.

"We didn't know what to do," she explained. "I was running circles around the snakes trying to confuse them, and Kozmo was swooping in with airborne attacks while Runt and Flicker tried to guard you, but it was still a losing battle. We knew it was only a matter of time before we lost the energy to hold them off, and with the snakes' venom, even one strike would be enough to kill. Kozmo came up with a brilliant plan to lure them away."

"To use me as bait."

Jazlyn's nose twitched in annoyance. "To divert the mass so we could split up and have a better chance at surviving. Luckily, thanks to Kozmo's quick thinking, we don't have to worry about them coming back at all now."

Castor took a long look at the bat-fox. She had pulled his tail, told lies about him to the snakes, and assumed he was dumb enough that he wouldn't figure out the scheme and blow her cover.

She'd also saved his life and, more importantly, those of the animals he cared about most.

He hung his head in shame. "Thank you," he said with a whimper, his tail hanging low. "I . . . I misjudged you. I'm sorry. I don't know how I can ever repay you."

Kozmo hugged her wings around herself shyly, and her own tail swished. "You just did," she answered.

44

THE DESERT NIGHT WAS COLD AND CLEAR, AND CASTOR lay on his back, looking up into the sky. He felt something shift next to him, and he flinched. His ears quivered, straining to hear more, to assess whether he or his pack was at risk.

But it was just Kozmo.

"Can't sleep?" the fox-bat whispered to him.

"I want to make sure nothing sneaks up on us tonight. It's so dark."

"I was actually thinking how light it is," Kozmo said. "Those stars are like a zillion fireflies. I've never seen anything like it. And there's so much space out here!"

"Yeah, space enough for predators to come at us from any angle," Castor muttered, anxious.

"Don't worry," Kozmo assured him. "No snakes out there this time."

"How can you tell?"

She let out a shrill screech, and Castor jerked onto his feet.

"Shhh!" he growled. "You're going to attract them!"

"Sorry," she squeaked. "I was just double-checking for anything giving off heat—my voice bounces back to tell me the distance. There's nothing out there for miles."

Castor settled back down into the pile. "That's pretty neat that you can do that, I guess." Maybe Kozmo wasn't so bad after all. "They all seem to like you better than me these days," Castor said after a beat. He could feel the warmth of the other bodies around him, but Castor still felt isolated. "When I wasn't paying attention, you snuck your way right into my family."

He didn't mean for it to sound like an accusation. Kozmo sounded genuinely surprised.

"Really?" she said. "I feel like you and Jazlyn are so close, and Runt and Flicker are best friends. Sometimes

I feel like there's no room for me."

She said it in a small voice, like she was nervous he'd tell her she was right, and Castor felt guilty for the way he'd treated her.

"I didn't mean to make you feel like that. I was just afraid."

"Of me?"

"Of everything," Castor barked bitterly. "I'm supposed to be a leader—this fearsome mutant dog, this winner. But really I'm the biggest scaredy-cat there is. You saw me today—so terrified I couldn't move. I couldn't protect my family. Runt . . ."

"Runt is fine. We're all fine. And I think it's okay to be scared. I've been scared my whole life, and it's what kept me alive. I think sometimes that being afraid, and just dealing with it, is what being brave is."

That sounded like something Pookie, his mentor, had told Castor before one of his first matches. Looking up at the twinkling stars, Castor thought of how Pookie's web had shimmered under the stadium lights, how he'd spelled out CASTOR THE BRAVE to give Castor courage each time he looked up. It felt like Pookie was with him now.

"There doesn't always have to be a leader, you know," Kozmo continued. "Or a winner. I feel like we just have to do what we can for each other, when we can." She paused, thoughtful. "It's better than being alone, which is what I was before."

She was shivering a bit next to him, and Castor draped one of his long wings over the fox-bat.

"None of us have to be alone anymore," he said, finally believing it himself. "We're all part of the same pack now."

45

MARCUS AND LEESA CROUCHED BETWEEN SCRUBBY WEEDS and strewn trash on Reformers Island, where the NuFormz facility was located. They were about a half mile from the entrance to NuFormz, and together, they anxiously watched the road that wound down the ridge to the city center. They were waiting, but neither of them was exactly sure what for yet. A sign? An arrest? A rescue?

Suffice to say, the break-in didn't quite go as planned.

Stealing Pete's aircar had been a piece of cake, and despite his guilt, Marcus had even let Leesa control it on the way down the steep slope. They'd made it onto the island a-okay!

Sadly, that was where their good luck had ended.

Since Pete had been fired and was now being prosecuted by NuFormz, they'd already deactivated all his access, including the code to slide the car into port, which was also their building access. At the last minute, Leesa had convinced Marcus to abandon the car and jump, so now they were stuck on an island under government lockdown, without a way into the building, without a mask to protect themselves against the elements, and without a way off the island other than the wheels of his skateboard, which he'd grabbed at the last minute.

Marcus could see other aircars gliding down the cable lines, and above them hele-pros chopped at smog, but here at ground level, the road leading to the island was empty. They were in a bad spot, that was for sure. The temperature outside was already climbing to dangerous levels.

They had met at ten, when the Skypark opened (which was where he'd told his mom he was going), and they had really gone to the park first, all so he could show off a few skate tricks to Leesa. She'd actually clapped, which seemed like the greatest thing ever, but now that he saw Leesa's tan skin starting to burn and his fairer complexion already blistering in places, he wished they'd made a different call.

Or scrapped this whole crazy plan in the first place.

This is why we have rules about daylight exposure, he could almost hear his mom chiding. She was going to lose it when she saw him. If he made it home . . .

He was probably being dramatic, but he could tell Leesa was nervous, too. Her fingers worried at a piece of grass, slowly shredding it while she studied the road.

"There!" she said suddenly, pointing to a white box passing the roadblock and coming across the bridge. "There's our savior!" She was actually laughing now, shaking off the nerves. She had a nice, easy laugh. And cute dimples.

When it finally rumbled past, Marcus grabbed Leesa's hand and together they sprang out of the weeds and slipped behind the truck, crossing their fingers that the driver wasn't paying attention to his side mirrors. It was going slowly enough that Marcus was able to boost Leesa onto the back bumper. It got away from him after that, though, and Marcus had to kick fast on his skateboard to catch up. He made it in the end, though, and by the time he joined Leesa on the metal ledge, she'd already pried open the rusty metal latch.

The inside of the truck was louder than the Dome during a Mega Mash-up, and that was really saying something. The monkey shrieked. The kangaroo kicked at the sides of its cage. The cats hissed and meowed and moaned. Only the vulture watched in silence.

"Why would they be bringing new nonmutants in if the Unnaturals games are done?" Marcus shouted over the racket. Seeing the new animals in cages made him sick to his stomach. They were all so panicked and afraid. Marcus made a split-second decision and unclipped a carabiner from his belt loop.

"What is that?"

"A skate tool for tightening wheels or ball bearings. I think it'll work as a key."

He started to work the small wrench into the lock on one of the cages. Leesa pursed her lips in doubt, but the lock on the cage had popped open, and a kangaroo surged out feet first.

"Okay, so maybe that wasn't the best idea," Marcus admitted five minutes later, as they were dodging the animal's kicks.

"Ya think?" Leesa said, ducking behind the capuchin monkey's cage. It screeched in agreement.

The driver must've heard the commotion in the back, because he slammed on the brakes, and the cages crashed against the door. Many of them burst open, and the animals inside rushed out, frantic. Now the kids were trying to avoid a beak in the eye or a horn to the face.

It was only for a moment, though. They heard someone fumbling with the latch. The door opened, and it was Horace, the red-faced training manager that Marcus had seen mistreat the animals.

"You!" he bellowed, recognizing them right away.

Marcus clutched the tool in his fist defensively, but luckily, he didn't have to use it. Balancing on its muscular tail, the kangaroo launched its legs forward, slamming its feet into Horace's broad stomach.

Following the fleeing animals, Leesa and Marcus stumbled around overturned cages and strewn feathers and jumped out of the truck. It was parked inside the garage, and they sprinted to the door to NuFormz, dreading the new horrors they might find inside.

46

MARCUS KNEW HIS WAY AROUND THE BRIGHTLY LIT HALL-ways of the island prison—Pete had snuck him in quite a few times to see his favorite Unnaturals, the Fearless and the Underdog, when they'd been hurt. As they neared the corner before Bruce's private office lab, Marcus motioned for Leesa to slow down. Sure enough, he could hear Bruce's grim voice, having a heated conversation with another guy.

"I hear you paid off Horace to bring in new animals

for your little experiments. That's not going to go over well, I bet. She *told* you no more newbies. What happens if some nosy journalist has got eyes on the place?"

"That's Vince!" Leesa whispered. "I recognize the voice."

"We just need a few more test mutations to get the serum right. Please."

Bruce now, sounding desperate.

"End of the week. That's all you have."

"I'm in charge here," Bruce said in whiny irritation—this was the tone he usually used with Marcus at home. "I say when the trials are over."

"Nah, old man. Mayor Eris is in charge, and Ms. Eva prefers to go directly through me now. You could say I got a promotion. And once my Clan finds Francine, you'll probably be calling me Boss."

"Francine is the mayor's daughter," Leesa told Marcus.

"She's missing?" he whispered. Leesa shrugged, straining to listen.

"I just need a bit more time. I've spent years working to help that child," Bruce snapped.

"Lots of good it's done so far."

Vince's voice was still light, but there was an edge to it when he answered, a finality. "End of the week, Doc.

Then we move to H-trials."

"This is unethical!"

The sound of Vince's laughter.

"I want out, okay? You tell Eva I want out."

More laughter, the slam of a door, then the sound of Vince's steel-toed boots echoing down the hall.

Leesa wiggled her eyebrows, and Marcus knew she was wondering the same thing he was: *What exactly was going to happen in one week?*

"I won't do it, I won't do it," the kids could hear Bruce muttering inside with increasing agitation. "I'm done. ENOUGH!"

They heard the sound of a glass shattering. And then another.

"The vials of serum!" Leesa hissed.

"We have to go in there!"

But when he reached for the doorknob, it was locked. Marcus started to jiggle the handle.

"Hello?" Bruce's voice asked, high and fearful, from the other side. "Who's there?"

Marcus didn't answer—if Bruce knew it was him, there was about a zero percent chance he'd let them in. Marcus jiggled the knob more forcefully in response, and the door rattled on its frame.

"Vince? Mayor Eris? Is . . . is that you?"

Leesa started to pound on the door now, and inside, they could hear Bruce scrambling to his feet. As soon as he opened the door, Leesa pushed past him, and Marcus was face-to-face with his stepdad.

"Marcus?" Bruce gasped. "What are you doing here?" His eyes were wide and a flush crept up his neck.

Marcus glanced around him at the equipment strewn on the long metal tables. Test tubes, mixing dishes, microscopes, goggles. The room looked like what he'd always imagined school science labs to be a long, long time ago, before learning relied so much on slipstreaming and virtual experience. Apart from the broken glass on the floor, anyway. Leesa was right—Bruce had been destroying the vials of serum. Bruce rushed to grab anything he could and shove it out of sight. His usually precise movements were erratic, his hands fluttering around him like birds.

But Leesa was already marching across the room toward the trays of test tubes.

"We know all about the serum," she said, and Marcus was in awe of how confident and in control she sounded. "We know what you and Eris are planning." She was way better at bluffing than Marcus was.

Bruce's face spasmed in panic. "Oh, God, the press has already found out, haven't they? I'm ruined." His eyes were red rimmed and wild, his glasses askew. He ripped them off his face and started polishing them frantically with a dirty cloth as he muttered under his breath. "I thought it would work. *Tigris scorpiones* was always the most robust hybrid in matches. Certainly stronger than *Vulpes pongo chiroptera*. So why won't the hominid cells adapt?"

Marcus used to know a lot of the official names from researching animals during his Unnaturals fandom. *Vulpes*—that meant bat, right? And he recognized *Tigris* as tiger from the Invincible. Other than that, though, Marcus had no idea what Bruce was talking about.

"We were trying to save the world! You and your brother always thought I was such a bad guy, but I always tried to do the right thing—you could never see that."

Marcus couldn't help but scoff. "You thought the right thing was creating animals that would be hurt and killed for entertainment?" Bruce didn't exactly make it easy to like him.

"De-extinction was about *saving* animals, not destroying them. It was always about the research, never the glory." He laughed bitterly. "Now she's threatening my own kids?"

Marcus hadn't heard Bruce refer to him and Pete as his kids before. It made him feel weird—maybe because of all the things Bruce had said, that was the one thing that made Marcus feel like he'd gotten him wrong, somehow. And it sounded like he and Pete were in danger?

"Where's Pete?" he asked, cutting to the chase.

Bruce's fake smile fell, and he sank onto a stool with a deep sigh.

"Just tell us! I know you know."

"He's basically a hostage," Bruce said dejectedly. "Eris's hostage." He slumped forward, and his shoulders shook as he started to cry.

Marcus blinked. *A hostage? For what? Why is the mayor blackmailing Bruce?*

"What does she want you to do, Bruce?" Marcus pressed.

"I truly believed I could help the girl. Help all of us. But the experiment has changed. There are too many variables. It's over."

He jumped up and started pacing, and then he got this crazy look in his eye and lunged for a Bunsen burner. Cranking on the gas, Bruce lit a match and started feeding papers and anything else within reach into the flame.

"Bruce?" Marcus asked nervously. "What are you doing?"

"I have to destroy it. Them."

Bruce was reckless and frantic right now, and waving

that flame way too close to various chemicals and powders. There was a sudden spark and a small explosion that threw them to the floor.

Bruce was against the wall, and he screamed as a paw darted out, scratching his arm. The cages had been covered with a curtain—Marcus hadn't even realized there were animals in here with them!

Leesa was crouched near the line of animal cages. "He has more scorpion-tigers in here," she gasped, looking past Bruce to meet Marcus's eyes. "They all look just like the Invincible!"

By the time they understood what was happening the flames were licking higher and higher. The scorpion beasts were yowling and pacing as the smoke filled up their cages. They were just innocent animals! They didn't deserve to die like that.

Marcus stumbled over, coughing, and started undoing the latches, not thinking about the fact that they were bred to kill anything in sight.

The scientist understood in the moment before Marcus did what was about to happen, though, and right as the stinging cats burst from the cages, claws swiping and fangs bared, Bruce threw himself over Marcus's body, shielding him from the deepest scratches, as smoke enveloped them both.

47

THE LONG-SUFFERING MUTANTS WERE ABOUT TO RETRACE their steps through the desert when something caught the corner of Kozmo's eye, like glass reflecting the light. Was that . . . a ripple of a wave? A flash of water? Or a trick of the sun?

Flicker had said it was a mirage before, and Kozmo didn't have the best eyesight, especially during the day. But now Castor was standing beside her, squinting in the same direction.

"Flicker knows where she's going," Runt yipped. He and the lizard were already a ways ahead. "We just have to trust her."

Flicker seems to know a lot of things, Kozmo thought. But none of them really knew what went on inside that scaly head. "What's it smell like to you?" she asked Castor, putting her trust in him first for once.

"It smells like water," Castor said immediately. "Might just be my brain wishing it was water, though," he admitted. "What do you think?"

"I think the sun sets in the west," Kozmo answered. Old habits die hard, and she'd replaced her fluorescent-light-tracking routine of the room with a sun-tracking routine in the desert. Each day she noted its progress across the sky, what time it went to bed, and what time it got up in the morning. The days weren't getting longer after all, even though it felt that way.

She could tell Castor didn't get the connection, though. "The west? Huh," he said, cocking his head toward the circle of yellow overhead.

Kozmo picked up a spindly stick in her muzzle and started to draw in the sand. "Jazlyn said that when she was in the science classroom, she learned that the only thing to the east of the city was barren wasteland." She marked the wasteland on the right side of her map. "According to the sun, that means the wasteland is behind us."

"It's hard to believe anything is worse than this desert, but okay, avoid barren wasteland," Castor said. "Check."

He still wasn't getting it.

"So, if the barren wasteland is to the east of the city, that means that the river is to the west, and the Greenplains are farther west beyond that. And according to the sun, west is over there." She nodded in the direction Castor had been pointing his nose. "Which means . . ."

"It *is* the river I smell!"

Finally, he got it.

Castor's tail stopped wagging suddenly as his face fell. "And it means the Greenplains are way back there, in the opposite direction." Castor stood and looked after the group. "We'll be right back." He howled to throw his voice.

"Wait!" Flicker was dashing toward them, sand whipping up in all directions so that she looked like she was running on water instead of hot ground. None of them had ever seen the lizard move so quickly before! "Don't go over there, whatever you do! It's quicksand. And full of mirages. And, um, infested with tarantulas!"

"I happen to love tarantulas, anyway," Castor said. The way Flicker was talking made Castor suspicious. He turned to his friend. "Jazlyn? Can you come take a look at this?"

Castor whispered to her for a minute, and then, after giving them a strange look, the rabbit-panther raced toward the shimmering distance, careful to avoid the quicksand pits. She was back in less than a minute, and confirmed their suspicions.

"I could see the outline of the trees, way down the river," she reported, eyes wild. "How are we so off course?"

Runt's eyes were wide and watery, his head cocked in a curious pose. "We're not going to the Greenplains?" he asked, his voice small. "Flicker?"

Now the lizard was looking pale in the gills and green with guilt.

"Have you even been to the Greenplains?" Castor's voice was a sharp bark this time.

"Yes!"

Jazlyn stepped forward, shoulder muscles rolling. "Then you *knew* that you were taking us in the wrong direction? Far north of Lion's Head, when we should've been going west, just across the river? We must be fifty miles away."

She pulled herself up tall to glower at Flicker, and for the first time, Kozmo could see how fearsome the rabbit-panther really was.

"You *lied* to us!" she said with a hiss. "*Why?*"

Flicker looked down at the sand. Her eyes tracked in opposite directions, noncommittal. "I thought . . . I just wanted an adventure and . . . a friend . . . and I . . . I'm sorry."

It was then that Runt sat down in the sand and began to howl.

48

In a strange turn of events, Marcus was going to stay with Leesa. In her one-room apartment. In the Drain. Underground. And for some reason, she was totally panicking about it.

It's fine, Leesa told herself as they descended. *Don't be weird about it. He'll know if you're being weird about it. Just helping a friend in need.*

Never in her life did Leesa think that Marcus's mom would be calling her mom and asking if her son could stay with them for a few days. From what Marcus had said when they'd first met, Leesa got the sense that he'd only been allowed below the 100th floor line a handful of times. Clearly, the woman must've been desperate.

Marcus's stepdad, Bruce, had basically gone mad scientist, in the really nutso sense, right in front of them in the lab. They'd managed to get the guy home in the aircar, but then Bruce had to go to the hospital for the tiger-clone scratches, and when he'd started babbling about performing sacrifices for the red queen and resurrecting a zombie woolly mammoth, the doctors said they were going to keep him there for a while. Leesa was pretty sure it involved padded walls.

Marcus's mom was staying by Bruce's side for the time being, and Pete was still missing, of course. Marcus said he was obviously old enough to stay home by himself, and Leesa pointed out that Zippy the automopooch could babysit him, which he didn't think was half as funny as she did. But apparently his mom thought that leaving her almost teenage son in an all-white, all-glass apartment was riskier than sending him underground with potential viruses and bad influences, because he'd gone home to load up a backpack, and now here they were, about to descend into the Drain together.

"It's this way," Leesa said, gesturing for him to follow

her down the stairwell, and then immediately felt foolish. It was pretty obvious how you got to the Drain, wasn't it? Maybe not. For all their fancy educations, sky kids seemed to know surprisingly little.

This wasn't a *sky kid*, though. This was Marcus, and he was smart. Marcus seemed to have forgotten to pack his wit in that big backpack today, though, because as soon as they were underground, he started saying the dumbest, most obvious things she'd ever heard.

"It's, like, a real neighborhood. A real city, with streets and homes and everything."

"Yeah . . ." Leesa smiled awkwardly, trying to give him the benefit of the doubt. "What'd you expect? That we'd all be mole people or something?"

"No, no, of course not," Marcus said quickly.

But from the tone of his voice, Leesa could tell that he kind of had. It went downhill from there.

"There are so many people."

"Mmm," she'd answer neutrally, while inside her head, she was yelling, *Yes, over three-quarters of the population is crammed under the street so that you can all spread out and stretch your arms in the clouds.*

"It's so dark."

That's because there is no sun underground and all the light is piped in.

"The center is so lively."

Yeah, because this is where people shop and talk and work and trade and live!

"I can't believe there are trees."

Technology, filtered light, photosynthesis, oxygen, survival. Science! What do you want from me?

"The architecture is so creative."

It's called having not a lot of space, not a lot of materials (mostly junk that you guys don't want), and a whole lot of families trying to make it work. That's how you end up with stacked subway-car towers and tent cities made of trash.

And finally, the most genius comment of all: "It's so different from the Towers."

"NO KIDDING!" She whirled around on him, red faced, finally fed up. "Yes. I get it. It's way different than the sky luxury you're used to. It's obviously not light and airy and full of rich people and fancy things and solid structures with the best, sleekest, prettiest materials! It's a neighborhood of people who had a tough break and got shoved underground and out of sight and totally forgotten about."

"Whoa." Marcus's pale face blanched paler, so it looked almost green under the fluorescent light. "I didn't mean—"

She didn't care what he meant. He'd already had his turn to talk. "But it's still full of lots of *good* people who care about their neighbors, and their homes, and their work."

"I know," Marcus cut in. "Leesa, I know."

"You *don't* know. You don't know what it's like to grow up in one room with no windows and just a futon to share and a mom who is working so hard and a dad who's not even there."

"Yes, I do." He smiled gently, a sad smile. "At least that last part. And I know it sucks."

His dead dad. Shoot. Leesa felt awful for saying that. She wasn't done making her point, though.

"A lot of it sucks. But I'm still proud of where I grew up. I *like* being from here, *okay?*" For the first time, she realized it was true. She understood her mom's hopes of a better life and getting out of the tunnels someday, but this place had shaped who Leesa was.

"Okay!" Marcus grinned.

Leesa's face was flushed, and her heart was thumping quickly. A group of old ladies selling their market goods had turned to stare and were clicking their tongues at her.

"Okay," Leesa said, a little quieter.

"For what it's worth"—Marcus nudged her shoulder— "I wasn't judging where you come from, or any of this.

It's different, but in a good way. It feels like a different country. I kinda like it better."

Leesa snorted and rolled her eyes. "Yeah, right." But she felt better. Her breathing didn't feel quite so tight in her chest. She tugged one of Marcus's backpack straps and turned him down the alley that led to her apartment.

She opened the eight locks as quietly as she could, knowing that her mom was probably already taking her nap between her shift as a sky assistant and her job at the factory. But the last dead bolt always jammed, and by the time Leesa finally heard it *click* and pushed open the door, her mom was already sitting up on the futon, blinking the sleep from her eyes.

"Mom, this is Marcus. Marcus, Mom."

Her mom stood up, quickly smoothing her clothes. Their house might've been tiny, but she kept it spotless, and she always looked perfect, too. It was the first thing you noticed about her—her style. Leesa never got sick of showing her mom off.

Leesa's mom strode over and held her hand out to Marcus. It was a little formal, but Marcus shook it enthusiastically.

"So, you're the boy my daughter's been sneaking off to see all the time and who got her in all that trouble."

"Um . . ."

Leesa got a kick out of how flustered Marcus looked.

"Just kidding." Her mom let out a deep laugh that filled the room. "I know she finds trouble just fine on her own. I hear you're sharp enough to make Leesa laugh and stubborn enough to give her a run for her money. Both are pretty rare, you know."

"Okay, okay," Leesa said, blushing.

After setting up Marcus's sleeping bag—good for below freezing, even though they lived in a heat zone!—giving him a tour with the history of every tchotchke and trinket, and asking him about every detail in his life, Leesa's mom headed out for her second shift, and they were alone again.

"Oh!" Leesa said. "I almost forgot." She went to get the notebook and brought it back to Marcus.

"Is this Bruce's?" he asked, turning it over in his hand.

Leesa nodded. "I grabbed it in the lab when the fire started. Bruce seemed pretty unhinged, and I thought there might be something important in there." She scooted closer to him on the futon so they could look through it together.

The scrawl was mostly equations that were pretty far over their heads, but there were a few things in the margins that set off alarm bells and victory horns all at once—things like *Unnaturals as prototype, L1 most aggressive, backup Laringos, need to control,* and something about K-group.

"K-group," Marcus said. "Isn't that . . ."

"What Pete said the researchers were talking about!" Leesa said, nodding. "And look here." She pointed to another page where *K-group* was written next to *Vulpes pongo chiroptera.* "Wasn't that what Bruce had been muttering in the labs?"

"Fox-human-bat," Marcus said. "I looked it up after. But what's this?" He turned to a graph on the next page. One column was labeled *TOLERANCES.* It listed things like *solar, pollutant,* and *predators,* and the opposite column—*GROUP NO.*—had a bunch of letters listed. The weird thing was, after *K,* which had *deceased* written next to it, all the letters had been crossed out and *Kill Clan* had been written over them again and again.

What did all that mean, though? Marcus leaned close to study the graph, and Leesa was sure he could hear her heart beating.

Leesa's phone dinged. Antonio. Ugh, he was always trying to ruin everything.

Enough. Leesa clicked the sound off.

"That, um, your book about the detective girl? Nancy . . ." Marcus leaned even closer to her as he tried to decipher the cover of the paperback from Ms. Hoiles she'd left sitting on the table.

"Drew. Uh-huh. We should go over the clues!" Leesa stood up quickly, hoping he didn't notice when she wiped her sweaty palms on her jeans, and went to get her tablet to take notes.

She made a list.

THE SERUM: a virus that makes animals mean; they're making it in bulk; Bruce thought he was protecting people by making it, but now he regrets it.

THE VIDEO OF PETE: a distraction that makes the citizens think this is a small operation; suggests something bigger; proves there is a real reaction with the serum that makes the animals even more violent toward people.

FRANCINE: the mayor's daughter, who she will do anything for; very sick, tried to move to Paloma to get better, but was denied entry; missing.

KILL CLAN: test subjects in Bruce's notes; what the serum creates; part of Vince's plan to start a revolution.

THE INVINCIBLE CLONES: Bruce created them thinking they'd be even better than the Kill Clan—"more robust."

THE "GREATER GOOD": what the mayor thinks she's working toward; says that you have to compromise and do bad to save the world; talks about wanting to protect citizens.

K-GROUP: a fox-human-bat; Bruce thinks it's dead, Pete said it's alive; important in Bruce's notes.

"It's still not enough," Marcus said, shaking his head. A long blond strand fell forward, and he tucked it back behind his ear. "All of that is just stuff we've heard. Almost none of it is actual evidence."

Leesa fished a vial of serum out of the front pocket of Marcus's backpack. "This is."

Marcus looked impressed that she'd managed to swipe it from the lab during all the commotion. Leesa felt pretty proud of herself, too.

"Okay, but what are we going to say when this story breaks? Pete said this is something bigger, but are we any closer to figuring it out?"

Leesa added two more items at the bottom.

UNNATURALS: entertainment to distract the citizens of Lion's Head while Bruce and the mayor are using them as test subjects for the serum; *cover story!*

REAL STORY: ???

Then they stared at it for a really long time, offering ideas that seemed completely unbelievable, like the last one Marcus tossed out.

"What if . . . What if the mayor is building an army?" he asked, rubbing his temples. They were both tired of thinking but too hyped up to go to sleep.

"An army?" Leesa yawned.

"Antonio told you it was the Drain's turn, that the underclass was about to rise up and take over. He said the word 'revolution,' and somehow the mayor was part of it. For a revolution, you need a force, right?"

That didn't make sense to Leesa. Wouldn't it be more obvious, with soldiers training and stuff? "I haven't noticed any groups of people gathering, have you?"

"I don't know," Marcus sighed. "I mean, there're people everywhere down here, all mashed together."

"Well, pardon us if we don't have airy condos to spread out in," Leesa snapped testily.

"Come on, that's not what I meant."

She waited.

"For starters, I don't mean a human army. I mean the mutants—a bunch of animals created to be strong, altered to be aggressive, and trained to attack on command. That would be enough to take control, right?"

Leesa propped up her head on her arm, considering.

"But why? Eris is already in control."

"Yeah, but things are shaky. You've seen the head-lines. The overcrowding, the lack of food. People are angry, and the matches worked as a distraction for a little while, but . . ."

"But now they're starting to blame the mayor," Leesa finished his thought. The idea was starting to make sense to her.

"Mayor Eris is part of the sky class, though—that's what I don't get. She built our Towers and picked the people to go in them."

Leesa remembered too well. Hers had been one of the families kicked out of them when the rent got too high and Eris held gambling debts over her dad's head.

Marcus continued. "Why would she turn on them to protect the Drainos?"

"Maybe she's not protecting us. Maybe she's protecting herself. Vince can be very persuasive. And like you said, things are shaky. I don't know how many rich sky people are trusting enough to follow her. But I could name quite a few Drainos desperate enough to follow Vince."

As if on cue, there was a sudden pounding on the door that made them both gasp.

49

It all happened in less than a minute, and it left them speechless afterward.

The banging on the door was so loud it sounded like someone was about to knock it right down, and in those first few seconds, Leesa was about as scared as she'd ever been in her whole life. Then she recognized Antonio's voice, yelling her name.

"Antonio, what the heck?" she asked as she yanked open the door.

He was already shoving past her into the small space. Leesa was worried he was sick or something, the way he was pacing—agitated, sweaty, like maybe he had a fever. But then he saw Marcus sitting on the futon, and he stopped dead in his tracks.

"I heard you brought him here. For what? Just to throw it in my face?"

Marcus was shrinking down into the cushions, his eyes wide as saucers. Leesa didn't blame him—Antonio had shot up in height this year, and she knew he'd been doing gym reps with Vince's friends every week. Paired with his threatening posture, it was pretty intimidating.

Leesa, on the other hand, had known him long enough to know that his bark was a whole lot bigger than his bite.

"Throw what in your face? There's nothing to throw." She tried to say it nicely, but like her sad gambler father, Leesa didn't have much of a poker face, and it was pretty clear she was furious. "We're *friends*, Antonio, and this is *my* house."

"I just don't get why you'd want to be seen with some sky kid instead of me." He was actually crying now, which Leesa was even less prepared for than the yelling. It actually made her madder. She was not going to feel sorry for him—not after how he was acting.

"And I can't believe you'd want to be seen with the

mayor, or even Vince, considering the war they're planning."

Antonio knit his bushy black eyebrows together in confusion. "Huh?"

"With the serum?" She held up the tiny vial and shook it in front of him.

Antonio's eyes widened, and he stopped in his tracks.

"How did you get a hold of that?" he gasped. It was like he was staring at the biggest, shiniest gemstone in the whole world. He was totally mesmerized. "Is that the H-trial?"

"I know what Eris is planning, Tony. Marcus and I figured it out. And she's not going to get away with it. When we go public with this as proof, it's all over and—"

Antonio snatched the serum right out of her hand. Then he turned to run.

"Hey!" Leesa yelled.

Marcus was on his feet before Antonio got to the door, and he tried to block the exit.

"Give it back!" Marcus ordered, and the right side of Antonio's lip curled up into a smile that verged on a sneer. He didn't even wind up to give Marcus a warning. He just jabbed his fist forward with a sharp drive that caught Marcus squarely in the left eye and laid him out on the floor.

"Oh my God, Antonio!" Leesa yelled as he bounded out the door.

She bent over Marcus, who was wincing in pain and trying to squint. His eye was already almost swollen shut, and a purple bruise was starting to bloom.

Wow. Leesa couldn't believe Antonio had actually hit her friend. She'd known Tony since he was eight years old, and no matter how tough he acted, this wasn't him. It was like he was possessed. She couldn't imagine what was in that serum that would make him do something like that. Now, it looked like she'd never find out.

50

MARCUS AND LEESA WERE IN A PINCH. THEY KNEW SOME-thing awful was going to happen, and soon, but they had no idea how to stop it. Who did you turn to when you thought war might break out in the streets? The government. Unless the government was the one starting the war. Who did you ask for help when you needed it? Your parents. Unless one of your parents was involved. Who did you turn to when all else failed? An expert.

"You should've come to me earlier," Joni Juniper

responded when they texted her. "Meet me at Pete's apartment, and we'll go over everything."

They punched the button for 247 and Leesa felt her stomach drop as the elevator shot them into the sky. A moment later, there was a soft ding, and they got out on Pete's floor of the Skyrise, Marcus separated the dog-shaped plastic icon from all the jangling metal keys on the ring, and pointed it at the door. There was a soft *click*.

As they sat in the living room waiting for Joni, Leesa tried not to get caught up in the view of the sky, the clouds, the *stuff*. Unlike Marcus's apartment, it wasn't spotless and all the curtains didn't match the pillows and rugs and dishes. Pete hadn't done much decorating. There were sneakers tossed in corners, veterinary books, crumbs under the furniture—*real crumbs*, Leesa thought enviously, not just calories that came in a pill like she ate most nights—a few framed pictures. She reached for one of the two brothers, with Pete as a teenager with dorky glasses holding his arm around a white-blond little kid with a skateboard and a skinned knee. She couldn't believe that was Marcus!

Her hand brushed against one of the knickknacks on the shelf, and she saw it was an Unnaturals figurine of Pookie. The urge to pick it up was overwhelming. She rubbed the plastic segmented spider legs, and stroked the dog's chin with its wiry strands of silvery hair—Pookie had always closed his eyes in pleasure when Leesa did that.

"Maybe we should look around while we're here," Marcus said, and Leesa quickly dropped the figurine back onto the shelf. "There's a chance we could find something that will help us get him out of there."

While Marcus sacked the living room, Leesa headed to Pete's bedroom and started rifling through the drawer next to his bed. It was stuffed with papers—real, actual papers, like in the pages of her books from Ms. Hoiles—and some of them were really old. She found diplomas and essays and an old pair of glasses, pawing through them quickly until she found a clothbound stack of pages at the bottom.

She pulled out a thin black-and-white clipping, and the ink smudged under her fingers. It must've been all the way back when people used printers. She read the headline: "GREEN INITIATIVE PULLS FUNDING AFTER THIRD AGENT DIAGNOSED WITH CANCER."

Leesa stared at the words, feeling their significance mounting. Hadn't Marcus mentioned that his dad had died of cancer?

"Marcus . . ."

She showed him the clipping, and when their eyes

met briefly over the page, Leesa understood a lot more about Marcus than she had before. This was the darkness that hung over him, the thing that had shaped who he was.

And considering that Francine was also sick, it also might be a clue.

The bell rang and Marcus and Leesa started.

Joni.

"This is big, really big," she said, bursting into the apartment and shaking the dire mood. She had lots of equipment with her. Recording equipment, cameras, lights. "We've gotta go live!"

"We don't have any real evidence, though," Leesa said. She sat in a comfy chair in front of a pale blue screen Joni had arranged in the kitchen to look like a TV set.

"So what? Since when has the media relied on proof? You're sitting on the biggest scoop Lion's Head has ever seen. With a politician, the public is your best weapon, and we need to get way out in front of this story."

"We just say what we think is going on, then?" Marcus sneezed as Joni brushed powder over his nose, getting him camera ready, and Leesa suppressed a giggle.

Joni tapped the excess powder out and shook her

head. "You never tell them the ending. Just give them all the puzzle pieces, and they'll do the work and tell you what the big picture is.

Leesa smiled, and her lips felt sticky from the gloss Joni had swiped across them.

"Sorry about the black eye," Marcus said to Joni, and Leesa felt her fury at Antonio flare up all over again. "That's the reason we don't have any evidence."

"Don't be! I'm not covering it up, I'm actually accentuating the bruising a bit just to even it out. The purple looks great with your blue eyes."

Okay, now Leesa couldn't help bursting into laughter. It felt good to smile—things had gotten pretty heavy lately.

"I'm serious!" Joni insisted. "Injuries play great with viewers. A kid targeted by violence for standing up for what he believes in? You'll look vulnerable and trustworthy. They'll eat it up."

All this talk about the performance of it made Leesa feel uncomfortable. "We're not trying to manipulate anyone. We just want to tell the truth."

"Good. So be honest. Just do it in a way that makes people want to actually believe you."

"How do we do that?" Marcus asked.

Joni smiled her big, dazzling smile that had made thousands of people fall in love with her when she was just an announcer on a virtual reality show. "Just follow my lead."

"I'm Joni Juniper, here with some breaking news. We've received troubling reports about some very strange activity at NuFormz. Mega Media said it was shutting down the facility weeks ago when an animal escape put citizens in danger. Now eyewitnesses claim to have seen more animals going in, and reports of new testing being done. What does it mean, and when should you panic? Let's investigate.

"Viewers might recognize my guests, Leesa Khan and Marcus Lund, from a most-memorable ending to the Unnaturals season—and franchise. These heroic kids put their lives on the line to stop the awful mistreatment of the gladiator-like mutants, but now we've learned that they might know even more about the sinister history at NuFormz."

"Hi," Marcus said into the microphone.

"Hey." Leesa waved.

"Marcus, it is your brother who is being held responsible for the mistreatment of these creatures, correct?"

"Yeah. But what they said he did was wrong."

"To bring viewers up to speed, Mayor Eris claimed in a statement that Peter Lund was giving steroids to animals to make them more aggressive for gambling purposes."

"Pete doesn't even gamble. His boss made him give that shot, and told him it was a booster shot."

Joni turned to the camera. "We should note that in our ongoing series on NuFormz, at least one employee claims it was standard practice to give these shots to Unnaturals. Further, we've been able to obtain one of these so-called steroid shots, and according to an expert on genetics, this is *not* a steroid shot or a booster, but a serum to initiate mutation with a focus on aggression."

"Right," Leesa said. "They're basically making super-mutants that kill on command."

"But if the Unnaturals is no longer airing, who are they training these terrifying creatures to kill?"

Leesa raised her eyebrows. "Your guess is as good as mine, Joni. But I will say that I'm from the Drain, and there've been a lot of riots lately because of the bad living conditions."

"And the people in my Sky Tower are complaining, too," Marcus added. "About space issues, tax hikes, and environmental hazards. No one's really happy with the government right now."

"Not to mention the rising tension with neighboring Paloma, with its comparably low pollution and fertile land," Joni pointed out. "You heard it here first. A shady business, a terrifying mutation that could be arriving at your own front door, and a mayor on the defensive. Is your government planning a takeover on your behalf? Do you really want a war? We'll be right back."

51

THE GREENPLAINS HAD ONCE BEEN LITTLE MORE THAN A dream. Then it was a blip of hope, and finally, a goal. Now, looking across that hazy horizon, Castor felt like it was receding into pure fantasy. After the longest journey of his life, he was farther away from the Greenplains than he'd ever been.

Castor squinted back toward the desert. For the first time in a long time, he thought about his first few weeks at NuFormz, when he stayed on his own, away from the other animals. A lone wolf could reach the Greenplains in no time. He could stretch his wings and soar down the river on the wind. Without obligation, without anyone to hold him back.

And without anyone to lift him up when he was low, or share in his joy when he reached paradise. A dog needed his pack.

"We turn around then," Castor said.

"No." Jazlyn's voice was high and wavering. Castor could hear the stress vibrating in just that one syllable. "We can't just go back the way we came. Think of all that we've faced so far."

Apart from everything at NuFormz, there were Crushers and Claws, zombies and humans. *Snakes*, Castor thought, his breath quickening.

"We were strong when we started out, and lucky. I don't know about you, but I'm not feeling quite as lucky anymore."

Castor had never heard Jazlyn talk like this. Despite her habit of freezing in fear, his friend was always remarkably calm, relentlessly optimistic. Something about Flicker's betrayal had caused Jazlyn's mask of goodwill to crack.

"You don't want to go to the Greenplains, anyway," Flicker said.

"Of course we want to go," Castor snapped. The lizard was trying his patience. It was one thing to lead them so far astray, another to tell him what he felt. "I made a promise to my friends, and I'm going to honor it no matter what. You probably don't know what that's like."

"It's not what you think," Flicker said, curling her fat green tail around herself defensively. "It's dangerous. Even more for you than for me."

"What are you talking about?" Castor asked.

But Kozmo rushed forward to interrupt. "Something's coming," she warned. She let out a screech, listened as the echo bounced back to her. "Several somethings. Fast."

Castor squinted toward the horizon, and as the animals started to take shape, something about their movement reminded him of a past encounter.

"Laringo?" he whispered. "Again?"

Now that Castor had seen the tiger-scorpion seemingly die twice, he was starting to think he truly was invincible.

But when the animals got closer, Castor saw that it was not one, not two, but *five* more Laringos. Not just brothers, like he and Runt were. They *were* him. Each one had that same stride, the same tics, the same tracking movements, the same small smile. Same segmented tail, same white-striped fur, same icy eyes.

Clones.

The Laringo army stood on the ridge, waiting for them.

"Get Runt to safety," Castor told Jazlyn.

"We'll take turns flying over and dive-bombing them," Kozmo said.

Castor nodded, but he felt uneasy. He was familiar with how Laringo fought from the Dome. He knew the tiger's stalking stride, and could anticipate the moment the scorpion tail would rise up for the sting.

Still, though they might be able to take on one Laringo, even that was a real struggle. With an infinite number of elite fighters constantly coming at them? Castor worried they didn't stand a chance.

Before they could even plan a strategy to launch their attack, though, Flicker started walking toward the deadly mutants.

"Where are you going?" Runt howled.

"It's me they're after," Flicker said, flicking her tongue. "If I go with them, they'll leave you alone."

"But you'll be killed!" Jazlyn said with alarm. Whatever her misgivings about the lizard, she had too good of a heart to turn away from her. "You can't face all of them on your own."

"They won't hurt me," Flicker insisted. "Besides, it's time for me to go home. I wanted adventure, but I miss my family. My mom must be worried."

"Your mom?" Kozmo asked, cocking her head.

But Flicker didn't say anything more. She just threw her scaly arms around Runt's neck for one more hug, and then slithered toward the white cats waiting in the dunes.

52

MARCUS WONDERED IF BRUCE HAD SEEN THEIR FILM FROM his bed in the hospital, or if his mom had. He wondered if she'd be home when he got there, ready to give him a hug or fix him some dinner.

When the doors slid open, it wasn't his mom who was waiting for him. It was a man in black.

"The mayor is giving a speech," he said, by way of introduction.

"Yeah . . . ," Marcus said. "I know."

"She invites you to attend as her guest."

"Uh, that's okay," Marcus said. "I was just going to watch the stream with the City Speak."

"The mayor invites you to attend," the man repeated. There was something strange about his eyes. A cold dullness.

Marcus did what he was told and climbed into the back of an auto-hele without so much as telling his parents he was leaving.

Most of the mayor's speeches were delivered in her room and projected live onto the buildings. It was mandatory to listen—or at least it was hard not to, with speakers blasting the words on every block—but there were usually no people on-site.

This was different. Thanks to Joni's mega-clickbait-y exposé, the central square of Lion's Head was full of people wearing gas masks, hoping to get a glimpse of the mayor and get her to answer to the accusations.

The mayor stood inside a glass box piped with oxygen so that she could remain mask-free and address the people directly as she talked. She was wearing a long green dress that made Marcus think of leaves, and her red hair was raked back into a tight bun.

Just before she started to speak, Leesa appeared next to Marcus, hustled in by another one of the mayor's goons.

She looked at him with hope—maybe this was when things finally started to change?

Then Mayor Eris took the podium.

"In the last few weeks, there has been a lot of speculation in the media about my company and my character. I wanted to speak to you all today to set the record straight.

"I have heard the peoples' frustrations, and I know that many of them are rooted in fear. According to scientists, in the next five years, the environment will be so damaged that people will no longer be able to breathe the air, even with a mask. As a species whose movements are already so relegated to small spaces, this is understandably concerning. Environmental stressors have made food scarce, space scarce, and have contributed to crime and serious health issues.

"This is especially close to my heart, as my own daughter suffers from an extreme sensitivity to UV rays and air pollution that puts her life at risk.

"I am most elated to report that after years of tireless research, we are working toward a cure for her condition. And it is because of this breakthrough that I am standing here before you today to make a special announcement:

"Mega Media has been keeping something
secret from you. These young activists were
right—the Unnaturals matches were connected
to something bigger: answering Lion's Head's
biggest environmental concerns. Using the revenue
generated from ticket sales, our top scientists have
been working to develop a cure for environmental
intolerances.

"We are thrilled to announce that we are finally
moving to human trials, and the drug will soon be
available in pill form. INVINSIFY will make you feel
stronger and healthier than the longest reigning
Unnaturals champion. It is going to change the face
of our modern world!

"Please register today if you wish to volunteer for
a trial and be one of the first to experience a truly
liberated existence. Thank you."

Afterward, Leesa hung at the back of the crowd, unsure
what to think. Had she been wrong? It was starting to
look that way.

And did she want to be? Had she gotten more caught
up in solving the mystery than saving the people?

It sounded like the mayor might *actually* be able

to save people. How could that be anything but a good thing?

She heard the voice that made her rage and smelled the cologne that made her gag. Antonio.

"Hey, Leesa."

Leesa crossed her arms and looked away. She wasn't going to make a scene, but she had made it clear to Antonio that she didn't want to see him again. She *really* didn't want to hear him say he'd told her so right now.

"I wanted to introduce you to the mayor, Ms. Eris."

Leesa couldn't believe what she was seeing. Here was Antonio, this Drain kid. With his stolen shoes and his ratty shirt and his accent. Standing with the mayor. Like they were friends.

"We've met," Mayor Eris told Antonio.

Leesa smiled awkwardly, not knowing how to stand. She didn't want to talk to Antonio, and she had a million questions for the mayor, and she was also kind of worried she'd get arrested for Joni's exposé or something.

"Antonio was one of our earliest supporters," the mayor told her. "He was instrumental in taking the program to its next stage."

"If you want, I can show you around the facility sometime," Antonio said.

"Is my brother there?" Marcus cut in, as if he'd been the one Antonio was inviting.

"Yes!" Mayor Eris answered, laying her fingertips on his arm. "So sorry about that misunderstanding. With his expert experience and caring manner, Peter has been a valuable addition to the team, helping the animals transition into their new environment in the Greenplains."

"Great. When can we go there?"

The mayor laughed, like he was being cute or something. "How does now sound?"

She was probably being cute with her answer, too, but Marcus ignored that possibility. His answer was direct: "Now's good."

At the mention of Pete, Joni was definitely going, too. "I need to accompany Marcus as his stand-in guardian," she told the mayor.

"The children don't need a guardian. They have me. But you are welcome to join us if you'd like a tour. Tell me, Ms. Juniper, are you one of those method journalists? You know, the kind of reporter who feels she really has to experience a story to be able to make a genuine contribution?"

"To some extent . . ."

"Because I really feel that the community could

315

benefit from someone of your status checking out the facilities first and reporting, so that everyone can see that what we're doing really is going to change lives."

"You'd give me full access?" Now *this* was the biggest scoop of her life. Joni looked like she might actually start jumping up and down.

"Of course," the mayor purred. "The complete elite experience."

53

CASTOR COULD SEE THE RATS PICKING AT THE GARBAGE IN the reeds on the bank below them. They were pink and hairless, and you could see their organs glowing through their thin, translucent skin. He thought of the dogs he and Runt had fought on the dock. He could still remember the sizzling sound the husky's fur had made when he'd fallen in, and how the dark water had closed over the top of him, like he'd never existed at all.

But Jazlyn was looking at the toxic river water, her

pink nose twitching thoughtfully.

"You know how to build a nest, right, Kozmo? And Runt, I bet you've found a few uses for trash in the alley before. Castor, you fly along the bank and pick up anything that might be useful. I have an idea."

The Unnaturals' river chariot was an abomination made of plastic and string, rain barrels and solar panels. It had a warp throne and a nutri-cube bin, and the whole thing was finished off with a sail made of a laminated poster that said MONIAC 4 LYFE. It certainly wasn't going to be winning any beauty contests, but it stayed afloat. And once it caught the wind, the little raft could really move.

It sure was whipping today. The choppy water and fast-moving clouds suggested a storm might be brewing.

"Look out!" Kozmo screeched. "Rocks!"

They were already upon them, though, and as the sharp edges of the stones jutted up against the little raft, the animals were thrown and jerked around. Jazlyn carefully maneuvered them though the rapids.

"I miss Flicker," Runt sighed when the waves had settled. "She was such a good climber. She could've scampered right up that post and been a lookout. She would've warned us about those rapids."

"She didn't warn us about anything else, did she?"

Castor growled.

But Jazlyn, who had been angriest about Flicker's betrayal, now had a softer response. "Would you have listened? Would any of us? Maybe it's a good thing we didn't go straight to the Greenplains. Maybe it was better to let the dream live for a bit longer, to be prepared for . . . something less than paradise."

"I feel like at this point, I'm prepared for almost anything," Castor said with a laugh.

"What's that?" Jazlyn asked. Their first mate had gone into freeze mode—something else had scared her stiff.

Now what?

A pale pink blade sliced through the water. Then another.

"River sharks," Kozmo whispered.

"How?" Castor gasped. He thought of the water closing over the husky with a sizzle and a burp.

"The Yellow Six used to talk about natural mutations. Sometimes you just adapt to what the environment throws at you."

There was frenzied thrashing, making the raft rock, but the water was too dark to get a clear view of the shapes of the creatures lurking beneath.

Until one jumped up, arcing out of the water in a fantastic leap. Its nose was long and pockmarked. The teeth were serrated. Its eyes were gelatinous lumps dangling from its head.

Though it was hideous-looking, Castor was considering how Pookie would've been impressed with the acrobatic feat, when the shark crashed back into the water, taking a bite out of the raft on its way down.

The crew scrambled to shift their weight and redistribute sections of the raft, but they couldn't move fast enough. The sharks were swarming, dismantling the raft, piece by piece. Soon, their powerful jaws would be biting into Castor and his friends.

"Don't eat us!" Runt begged. "Please!"

The thrashing stopped momentarily, and below one of the pink fins, a concerned face bobbed out of the water.

"Eat you?" one of the sharks asked. "Why would we do that? We're not savages!"

"Yet you're in the middle of ripping our boat to shreds," Castor pointed out.

The shark scrunched his pocked snout. "It's suppertime. What else are we supposed to eat?"

Another swam over. "We feast on the garbage of Lion's Head. Your raft is such a nice balanced meal—a little salty, a little sweet, a little plastic, a little pulpy, with that added umami of pollution. It's delicious!" It grinned, and its rows of jagged teeth gleamed. "I especially love the sail, as I, myself, am a Moniac."

"Oh, me too! Me too!" Runt yapped excitedly. "And guess what? This is a really good surprise for you and I know you're going to love it and I can't wait for you to guess!"

"Is it a karaoke machine?" one suggested.

"No . . ." Runt's tail wagged in anticipation.

"Is it a roller skate? I do love eating anything with wheels."

"No . . ." Runt looked to the next shark, wiggling his brows.

"I am really bad at guessing," it said dejectedly, and its fin flopped to the side. Then its eyes lit up suddenly. "Ooh, ooh, is it a life-size statue of one of the Unnaturals stars?"

"It's better!" Runt panted. "Some of us were *real* Unnaturals stars. Castor and Jazlyn were both part of Team Scratch!"

"*You're* Unnaturals? Get outta here! Fellas, come here, we have celebrities on our river!"

More fins sliced toward them until the water surrounding the raft—or the raggedy scraps that remained of the raft—was dense with pale pink bodies. Pockmarked noses crowded the edges of the raft, and gelatinous, googly eyes peered up.

"Oh, wow! It really is the Underdog! I recognize the gray eagle feathers."

"And there's the Swift! I heard she can go so fast the track catches fire."

"Which one are you?" a river shark asked, nudging the bushy orange tail with his nose.

"I'm just a Kozmo," the fox-bat answered.

"Don't worry, Kozmo. I'm sure you'll get your big break someday."

"Didn't you hear?" Runt asked. "The matches are over!"

"What a tragedy!"

"It felt more tragic to see your friends get hurt and risk your life for humans' entertainment every night," Castor said dryly.

"But your talent was incredible!"

The awe in the shark's voice was flattering, and Castor puffed out his chest, despite himself. While he'd never enjoyed fighting, he did like to think he'd been pretty good in the ring. He and Pookie had certainly worked hard at it every night.

"So, guys?" Kozmo said. "Sorry to interrupt, but I think we're sinking."

Toxic water seeped up through the bite marks in the plastic flooring. As it sloshed near their feet, a fine smoke formed. It wouldn't be long before the chemicals in the water burned up through what was left of the raft.

The first shark they talked to cocked his head. "I feel so bad that we wrecked the traveling vessel of superstars. Where are you going? These gentlesharks and I will be happy to give you a ride."

"Really? We're, um, trying to get to the Greenplains?" Kozmo said it like a question—after such a long journey, none of them was totally sure they would ever reach their destination. Or what surprises and disappointments that destination might hold.

"We're having a reunion with the rest of our team," Castor explained. "The Enforcer and the Fearless? And maybe the Mighty?"

If they were still alive. Castor hoped saying the words aloud would make them come true.

"You're kidding! The Fearless? The sassy Grizzly is my fave! Can you tell her Al says hello? I am totally her biggest fan." The shark blushed. "I wept when the Invincible beat her."

"We all did," Castor said, sharing a meaningful look with Jazlyn. He knew they were both remembering the match when Laringo had almost killed Enza. It was the final straw after months of suffering that had made them decide to plan an escape.

"So you think you can take us to the Greenplains?" Jazlyn pressed.

"Oh, sure, the Greenplains! It's right on the way."

Finally, they could see the trees of the Greenplains directly in sight. Captain Castor and his crew didn't have far to go.

"Hop on," the sharks invited, and one by one, the mutants climbed onto the slippery pink backs. They clutched tight to the fins, and the fleet started to drift slowly downriver.

"It's too shallow near shore for us to drop you right on the beach." The shark carrying Castor gestured with its pointed nose. "Will you be able to make it from here?

The outlines of the trees were visible through the fog just across the river.

"It's so close," Castor said. "We can fly, I'm sure of it."

"I know I can take Jazlyn that far," Kozmo confirmed.

Castor turned to Runt. "Ready, brother?"

"Greenplains, here we come!"

Castor grabbed Runt by the scruff of his neck, and when they took flight, he felt a moment of total exultation. He found himself holding his breath as he flew over the island. He saw the squat gray buildings, the high electric fencing. From here, even the golden egg of the Dome stadium looked small.

The eagle-dog glanced behind him one last time. Lion's Head was all sharp lines and small compartments, the people boxed up tight. How strange that they thought they were keeping themselves safe, when man was the most dangerous animal of all.

He turned away from the city. Castor was ready to finally stop running. He was ready for a new journey to begin.

PART THREE

PARADISE OF PREY

"Mayor to City: 'I Can Save the World!'"

"INVINSIFY: 'The Miracle Drug' in Trial Stage"

*"Stampede in Central Square as Citizens Rush to
Volunteer"*

54

As the mutant animals flew across the river, the smog started to clear, and the sight of the shoreline was so shocking that Kozmo almost dropped out of the sky and into the river. It was like the land itself was breathing, and for the first time Kozmo realized what the word *paradise* meant. She realized how simple her dreams had been. How plain.

Kozmo released her grip on Jazlyn's shoulders, and they both dropped down to the ground. It wasn't a gravelly ledge, like she'd seen on the other side; her feet sank into the lip of cool white sand. Castor and Runt had landed a little farther up the shore, and Kozmo and Jazlyn climbed up onto jutting rocks to join them.

Before them was a vast jungle. For several minutes, no one spoke.

"I didn't realize leaves came in more than one shape," Castor murmured, as if afraid to disturb the peace of this place. He was right. There were broad, flat leaves as long as Jazlyn's legs. Delicate, springy leaves coiled as tight as Flicker's tail. There were leaves that looked like stars, leaves that looked like cat tails.

"Or color!" Kozmo added.

All her life had been lived in dull, muted shades: a white room under harsh light, a gray tunnel or pale sand. She had been the bright spot, the orange anomaly. But what she was seeing now was so pure, so saturated, that it almost hurt to look at it.

Rusty red bushes and neon yellow grasses. Not to mention the *green*.

The trees, the land, even the tree trunks were green, covered in different types of dense moss. There was a vine winding around one with great, green globes of berries dangling in bunches.

Castor buried his nose in them. "It smells so . . . alive."

"What do you think they taste like?"

He raised a furry eyebrow—a dare.

She bit down and the fruit burst inside her mouth. "It's sweet," Kozmo reported. "And it tastes like . . ."

Like what? It wasn't like anything she could remember. It tasted like the opposite of everything she had eaten in the tunnels, the things that thrived in the darkness.

"Like the sun."

Kozmo had spent so much time running away from danger, she never thought she could enjoy running. But it was different when you were running toward something. Without the tightness of fear, her legs felt light. Without the anxiety stealing away her breath, her lungs felt full. Kozmo thought she might be able to run forever.

Until she saw Castor take flight.

Flying in this place was even better than running. While Castor spread his long eagle's wings in a clearing where he could soar untethered, Kozmo sought out the cool forest. She dipped and dodged between vines. She played in shadows.

It was only when she felt like she'd covered every inch of it and her heart was going to beat out of her chest that Kozmo dropped back down to her feet. With her tail swishing back and forth through the leaves along the forest floor, she padded out to join her friends.

Jazlyn and Runt were in a meadow, watching Castor soar high overhead. Here, there were more colors, too— flowers bursting open into shades that hadn't even been named yet.

Kozmo brought her snout in to sniff one, and it snapped shut, its sticky serum spattering on the tip of her nose. It *burned*, and for the first time since they'd come ashore, Kozmo thought of Flicker's warning.

When Castor dropped down, Runt tackled him. "It's perfect! Isn't it so perfect, Castor?" he barked excitedly, licking his brother's face.

"It is," Castor yipped in response, sounding almost like a puppy. "You were right. It really is paradise."

55

WHAT WAS IT THAT OLD GRAY, THE PACK ELDER, HAD SAID about paradise, when Castor and Runt were just puppies?

In this new world, it only exists in dreams.

Well, Castor was living out his dreams. All his life, he had heard stories about the majestic place across the river, where nature ruled and humans didn't dare venture. He'd never quite let himself believe they were true. And even when he was flying across the river with the wall of trees in sight, a part of him thought it would all be a mirage, like an oasis in the desert—that he could keep flapping his wings forever and never reach it.

Yet here he was, feet firmly planted on the shore of the Greenplains at last.

It was as beautiful as promised. They were safe, and nothing had tried to kill them. Still, Castor felt unsettled by the things that Flicker had said. Maybe she was just trying to scare them? Maybe she just wanted this whole place to herself.

He saw that despite their celebrations, his friends looked a little nervous, too.

"Awfully quiet here," Jazlyn remarked.

That was it—the silence. It was total, and that made it eerie. Even in NuFormz, a highly controlled environment, you heard guards coughing or the buzz of lights, the creak of doors. And in the desert, where so few things were even surviving, they had still heard the rustle of other life—Kozmo had actually heard it several feet below the surface.

Here, there was nothing. It was like every tree, every blade of grass, was holding its breath.

"Where do you think everybody else is?" Jazlyn asked softly. She stood still, her long ears rotating out, and Castor could see her heart beat fast in her ribs, vibrating the sleek dark fur of her coat.

"Maybe it's all ours," Kozmo suggested. "I mean, how do you know anyone else is here? Isn't it quarantined off?"

"Back in the city, we saw the videos of NuFormz being emptied out," Castor explained. "They shut down the Unnaturals matches after our escape, and announced that all the other mutants were being brought here."

"Our friends." Jazlyn glanced at Castor.

That was the reason they'd come. When Castor closed his eyes, he could see Samken's many trunks hanging limp in defeat as the claw machine plucked him off the ground and carried him off into the sky. He could hear Enza's angry roars as she was returned to chains. They had promised their friends they would make it here, no matter how many obstacles they faced. Castor had hoped the whole team would be waiting for him, but if not, they would bring them back here. He owed them that.

But if his friends weren't here . . . where were they? And what was being done to them?

"Maybe the other animals are out playing some-where," Runt suggested brightly. "Maybe paradise is so big, they're all spread out."

"Maybe."

Castor couldn't help but think of Old Gray's words as

some kind of warning, now. He remembered the warning on Flicker's face, and the lizard's irrational desire to lead them away from a lush wonderland. Had Flicker really not told them more about this place out of strange malice? Or had whatever happened here been so traumatic that she couldn't bear to speak about it?

The fur on Castor's spine stood up, and his brother instantly sensed the shift. Months apart hadn't made them any less attuned to each other.

"What's wrong?" Runt asked anxiously.

"Nothing."

It *was* nothing, Castor reminded himself. *Nothing* had happened. There had been no threat, not one single reason to worry.

Castor shook out his coat and cleared his throat. "We should find a place to sleep before dark."

"We should stay in the meadow," Kozmo suggested. "I can't wait to hunt fireflies under the stars."

She inhaled the fresh, grassy scent of the air, and though Castor tried not to focus on it, the musky undertone of the moss and wet leaves smelled slightly rotten to him now.

"No," he said a little too sharply. Now the whole group felt his tension. "We should find shelter. At least for the first night."

At Kozmo's mention of hunting, a flash of a dream had come back to Castor—the nightmare he'd had before his fight with Deja. He'd been in the middle of a hunt when the perspective had shifted and somehow he'd become the prey.

Standing in the big meadow, in *paradise*, Castor shivered. Even with his closest friends surrounding him and a cathedral of trees standing guard, Castor felt vulnerable, exposed on all sides.

56

THE BAT HALF OF KOZMO SEEMED TO HAVE A HOMING
device for finding secret nooks and crannies. Just a little ways up from the rocks lining the beach, she located
the mouth of a cave, carved into the slope. Castor had
seemed on edge, and though the Greenplains seemed
perfect to Kozmo, she was glad she could help the group
find shelter.

It started to rain just as the animals were climbing
inside, and Kozmo made a few circles before settling

down onto a nice dry patch. Runt plopped down beside her, stuck his tongue out and folded his ears back in a dramatic yawn, and then lay his head on her shoulder. Kozmo curled her pillowy tail around him. Soon both Castor and Jazlyn had dropped down to join the pile as well.

They watched the water come down in sheets, and Kozmo was transfixed. "This is my first storm," she said softly.

Jazlyn leaned in closer. "It's nourishing the soil. The water will make things look even greener by tomorrow."

Fantastic. Kozmo's eyes twinkled. "It's beautiful."

She thought about how much things had changed for her. Kozmo had spent the first part of her life in dark solitude, clinging to security by the tips of her toes and screeching at anything that got too close. The ceiling of the room had even once seemed big to her!

Now, she saw that the sky was forever. Snuggled up in the warm pile of fur, she hoped that her friends were, too.

A short time later, she woke up to the animals around her snoring, thinking she could use a little snack. Traveling with all these other animals, Kozmo had been forced to get off her nocturnal schedule, but she still had night cravings sometimes.

Not having any desire to get drenched in the downpour, Kozmo set her sights within the cave. There were sure to be some tasty insects hanging out at the back in the damp dark.

Strangely though, as Kozmo ventured farther into the cave, it didn't get darker, but *lighter*. She noticed reflected light, and she started to hear voices—both animal and human.

Before, Kozmo might've run, or she might have investigated on her own, with only her own fear to guide her. Now, she was part of a pack. They needed her, and she could admit that she needed them, too.

She sounded a screeching alarm, throwing her voice around the contours of the cave, and soon her three friends appeared, anxious and alert. They huddled together and crept forward, inch by inch. Whatever this cave led to, Kozmo was grateful she didn't have to face it alone.

The voices and scents grew in intensity as they approached, and Kozmo was surprised to have a familiar feeling about all of it.

Around the last corner, the cave abruptly ended in a door with a strip of light streaming brightly from underneath. Looking at one another and taking a deep breath, they pushed it open.

"Vince and Horace!" Runt whined.

"Enza and Samken!" Jazlyn gasped.

"Leesa and Marcus!" Castor barked.

The animals were blinking under the bright lights and looking around in confusion, but only Kozmo understood what was going on, and she was the most shocked of all.

"This is . . . the room."

"Which room?" Castor asked, the hackles on his back rising as he took in the cages, the clamps, the rows of shots.

"The room where I come from."

Somehow, her journey had ended right back where she began!

57

AFTER FOLLOWING THE MAYOR UNDERGROUND, THE group walked though a metal door and stepped into a large white room. The smell hit Leesa first, and then the noise. There must've been hundreds of animals in there. Countless types of mutants, pressing their bodies against a chain-link fence along the wall to the right. Leesa looked around her in horror.

This didn't look like a health center, like she'd been imagining. It didn't even look like an army. It looked like a graveyard.

There were more cages, too, beyond the lab tables on the left side of the room. She recognized the grizzly-tiger and the octo-elephant from the Unnaturals teams locked up in two of the biggest cages.

"What are you going to do to them?" she demanded.

To her surprise, the mayor waved her hand dismissively. "Oh, we're done with them now. We're letting them run free in the Greenplains, just like you wanted. Isn't that sweet?"

She nodded to Horace, whose face was satisfyingly scratched up. The cats must've gotten to him after the kangaroo. He glowered, but obeyed the mayor. With the flick of a switch, a trapdoor in the wall opened.

"The cave leads right outside," the mayor explained.

Marcus couldn't believe it. "You're just . . . letting them go?"

"They were just the beta phase of the project—it's common practice to test on animals first before you put a new product in the marketplace. But we don't need them anymore. Now we've got you."

Marcus narrowed his eyes. He wasn't getting it yet, but Leesa was starting to understand. So was Joni, judging by the way her brown skin had gone ashen.

There were six scientists dressed in yellow scrubs,

yellow caps, and yellow masks. She couldn't tell who they were, or even if they were men or women, but they all gazed at her and Marcus with the same strange, detached look, assessing them from head to toe like you might look at ingredients to make a meal. It made Leesa's skin crawl.

Leesa's mind raced to add everything up in her head. The Unnaturals as trials. The importance of the winners. Bruce's guilt. Antonio's arrogance. It all blurred together. She couldn't make sense of it. All she knew was that she had been dead wrong, and it could have some awful consequences.

"We were wrong," Leesa sputtered, gripping Marcus's arm. "We were wrong about the serum. About everything."

Marcus was barely listening, and she followed his gaze across the room. The mayor had told the truth about one thing: Pete was not in jail, and he was, indeed, helping out with the animals. He was in the corner with a mop, cleaning up waste.

"Pete!" Joni said, running over to him. She shook his arm and looked up into his face, but he didn't seem to be responding. His shoulders were hunched, and he kept his head down. Even after only meeting him a couple of times, Leesa could tell he didn't look like himself. He looked . . . like a zombie.

"What's wrong with him?" Marcus called, his voice cracking. "Is he all right?" He didn't seem to want to leave Leesa's side, though, for which she was grateful.

"We want the same things, you and I," Mayor Eris was saying.

What else had she said? Leesa needed to start paying attention. She had a feeling her life might depend on it.

"Freedom. The opportunity to improve our position in life. The strong will to take things into our own hands. To beat the odds."

"What's inside the serum?" Leesa asked. Right now, that seemed like the only thing that was truly important.

"Oh, just a little specialty cocktail." The mayor smiled. "Bruce took the very best genes from our winners and shook them up. Add a dash of compliance, a pinch of aggression, and the human component—or *H* for short—and you have the perfect creature, able to survive in any environment!"

"Perfect?" Leesa repeated. She thought she was pretty happy as she was.

"Well, not yet. That's the goal. We have a few final kinks to work out first, but luckily we've already had hundreds of volunteers just since the speech this afternoon. The citizens are *very* excited. I promised Vince that the public of the Drain would get preference to start, though—he's been so helpful in orchestrating this, after all. And you, you lucky girl, you get to be first!"

"One of the first," corrected Antonio.

"Ah, yes. Antonio is a little overeager."

"By the way, thanks for slipping me that serum, Marky. Vince wanted me to wait until the trials were all done, but I wanted to be the first. No one is going to give you anything in this life, right? You have to take it."

Leesa gritted her teeth. He had said that to her once, too—it's what made her decide to try to set Pookie free. Now the words had a sourness to them.

"What does it . . . do?" Leesa asked.

"It makes you feel like a superhero! Right, Mayor Eris?" Antonio asked, his voice a little nervous.

The mayor didn't answer his question directly. Instead, she smiled with tight lips and laid her pale hand on Antonio's arm. "Why don't you find out and tell us, little man?"

"Antonio, don't . . ." Leesa started to protest, but Antonio brushed her off.

"Why? You don't want to be my girl. If you're ever going to go for me, I guess I gotta turn it up a notch. Cheers!"

Antonio threw back the vial in one gulp. "How do you like me now?" he asked. He made a fist and flexed, showing off his strength, but his smile faded to an expression of uncertainty. "I don't feel so good," Antonio murmured.

Just then, the main door to the lab banged open, and there was commotion as the animals behind the fencing caught the scent of something new. Vince strode in trailing six white tigers on leashes, their segmented scorpion tails arcing over their heads. Leesa recognized them as the Laringo clones she and Marcus had saved from the fire in Bruce's lab. A giant lizard lumbered a few steps behind them.

"Did you find her?" the mayor asked sharply.

Vince nodded, but his expression was grave.

"Well?" The mayor took a few steps toward the group, her high-heeled shoes clicking on the floor. "Where is she? Where's my daughter?"

"Uh . . ." Vince started.

"I'm right here, Mama," a voice said. The mayor was still craning her neck past Vince and the animals, toward the lab door, but the lizard stepped forward. "It's me, Francine."

Leesa gasped. *That* was Francine? In the hologram

346

Leesa had seen in the mayor's office, Francine was a skinny girl with light brown hair, bound to a hoverchair. This was a lizard. It had rough scales covering its flesh, a long tail trailing behind it, and a green body that was turning a bit paler under the mayor's shocked gaze.

"I'm okay." The lizard—Francine—blinked at her mother with warm, brown *human* eyes.

"Okay?" the mayor shrieked. She rushed over to her daughter. "Okay?! How is this okay? What happened? Who did this to you?" She glared at the scientists in yellow.

"We didn't give her anything," one of them said, holding up his hands defensively.

"We found an empty vial next to the bed in H-Ward after Francine disappeared," another scientist explained. "It was from one of the earliest trials, when Bruce believed the common chameleon was the most adept at surviving in earth's hostile environment. But the testing showed it wasn't hominid—human—compatible . . ."

"No kidding!" the mayor cried, gesturing at Francine's reptilian face.

"I drank the serum myself," Francine said, flicking her forked tongue. "Vince brought his brother into my room and was telling him about how lucky I was to get to try it first, how it would make everything better. I just couldn't wait anymore. I couldn't stay in that bed getting poked and prodded one more second."

Leesa glanced over at Antonio, wondering how long ago he'd been down here in the lab, how long he'd known what was really going on. But Antonio did not look well. He was hunched over clutching his stomach, shaking in pain.

"Antonio?" Leesa said, worried.

"What did you give me?" He looked at Marcus and Leesa accusingly. When he reached out a hand to steady himself, Leesa stared. Antonio's hand was starting to change. Before her eyes, his nails were growing into points—*claws*—and thick fur was sprouting along his knuckles and all the way up his arm. A black-and-white striped pattern was forming.

Marcus looked from the Laringo clones back to Antonio, making the connection. His face was white as a sheet.

"What's happening?" Vince demanded, rushing over to his brother. "Someone help him!"

The scientists in yellow looked at one another and started to back away.

"We need Bruce," the mayor said decisively. "He can fix this. He has to." Her voice was shrill with desperation, and there was a wild glint in her eye. "He'll just have to run more trials. Horace, please escort our *volunteers* to their beds, where they'll be comfortable until we can get him in here."

She was opening a door marked H-WARD.

"No," Leesa said, backing up. Horace was right behind her, and he grabbed her arms behind her back with one big hand. "NOOOO!"

He clamped his other hand behind Marcus's neck. Joni was still across the room by Pete, and she glanced toward the door like she was about to make a run for it. But the Laringo clones stalked toward her, and Joni's eyes blinked in terror. She obediently walked over to H-Ward, and Horace shoved them all inside before turning and heading back out the door toward Antonio.

"You're not taking him." Vince was crouched over his seizing brother, and he shook his head from Horace to the mayor. The look in his eyes was deadly. "You're never touching him again."

Horace took one more step toward them, but Vince heaved Antonio into his arms and ran toward the fence, yanking the gate open. As the Kill Clan mutants started to stream out of their pen and toward the open cave door, Vince fled the lab, and Horace retreated back into H-Ward, slamming the door behind him.

Leesa and Marcus tensed. Now they were trapped in the little room. It smelled like pineapple lotion and antiseptic. Each bed was fitted with restricting straps, and wires with suction cups dangled ominously from beeping machines.

Marcus was finally beginning to understand a lot of what Bruce had been babbling about in his lab. "So that's what it was?" He sneered at the mayor as Horace tightened the straps around his arms. "You were blackmailing Bruce into fixing your daughter? You did all this, caused all this pain, destroyed lives."

"No sacrifice is too great for a mother to make for her child," Mayor Eris snapped. When she turned back to Francine, her tone shifted back to fawning. "We're very close to finding the right mix to get you sorted though, aren't we, sweetie?" She smiled adoringly at the badly deformed girl. "Hop up into bed, now."

Francine shook her head. "Please, Mama, no more. The serum worked. I can go outside now. I'm *fine*."

"We're so close, sweets." Mayor Eris grabbed her daughter's scaly hand and dragged her toward the middle bed. "Especially now that we can run human trials with subjects who are your age, not to mention your species. With enough experiments on them, Bruce is bound to have a breakthrough!"

Leesa started to scream.

She didn't stop screaming when they strapped her to the bed or when they placed the suction cups on her arms. She kept right on screaming until her voice was hoarse, and by that time she couldn't distinguish her own voice from those of the few remaining caged animals crying out in the great white room.

58

THE DOOR TO THE CAVE OPENED UP, AND MUTANTS STARTED to rush out of the room. Some of them were dazed, others frenzied, but some seemed clear headed and were weeping with joy, shouting about being free.

Free? Was the Greenplains really theirs for the taking?

Castor plastered himself against the wall of the cave to avoid the stampede, and Runt and Jazlyn kept close behind him. Kozmo had flown up into a crevice.

It was hard to tell what that place was, or what was

happening. There were too many bodies squeezing past them through the door, a blur of horns and hooves. But they didn't see any saber teeth. Or trunks. Or striped bulls.

Where were their friends?

"We'll have to search inside!" Castor said.

"I can't," the fox-bat squeaked from the crevice above. "I can't ever go back to that place."

"But you're the only one who knows it. You're the most important creature to help us."

The most important creature. That was what the man Bruce had said about her once. She didn't trust him, not now. But she trusted Castor.

"Please," the eagle-dog begged. "They're my family."

"Then they're my family, too," Kozmo said, and swooped down from her perch, leading them back into the Room that was as familiar to her as breathing.

"Enza!" Castor barked at the top of his voice.

"Sammie!" Jazlyn called out.

Kozmo saw right away that the gate of the Kill Clan's fence was hanging open on its hinges. That explained the stampede. "Over here." She flapped toward the cages on the other side of the room. Sure enough, the grizzly-tiger and the octo-elephant were side by side in two of the biggest cages.

"I knew you'd come!" Enza said, starting to cry. For

an animal as big as she was, it sounded more like a kitten's mewl.

Jazlyn squealed as one of Samken's trunks reached out to her and pulled her into a relieved embrace through the bars.

"Is that the Mighty, the zebra-bull who was the only survivor of the Mega Mash-up last season and famous coach of Team Scratch?" Runt asked in awe. His nose was pointing toward a cage in a shadowy corner.

"Hey, team," Moss said with a snort. "About time you all showed up."

Their friends were alive! Alive and lucid and stuck in an awful human lab.

"We were coming back for you," Castor said quickly. "As soon as we had a clear path, we were going to find you, so we could all be together at last."

"So we're together," Moss said dryly. "Think you could get us out of here, hotshot?"

Kozmo was already flying over to the hook where Vince always left his keys. It took some fumbling—paws were not so adept at such a task—but soon she had sprung open their cages. When Castor and Jazlyn embraced their friends, Kozmo went along the row of cages, freeing the other animals. It was something she should've done long ago.

Each animal thanked her and made for the open door, and Castor started to follow, leading the group. Now they could all be free in the Greenplains. Together! "It really is paradise, Enza—green and fresh and big. We've seen it. I can't wait for you to see it!"

But the mutant grizzly's dark, round eyes were frantic.

"Castor, we can't leave them."

The eagle-dog's heart sank, and his pulse quickened. "Who?"

"The Whistlers have the boy Marcus and the girl Leesa. The ones who saved us. They're behind that door."

59

AFTER LEESA HAD STOPPED SCREAMING, THE KIDS LAY IN H-Ward in silence for a few minutes, each wrestling with his or her own thoughts and fears. Marcus realized this might've been the first time in his life that he was truly afraid. He'd taken risks before, with skateboarding tricks and sneaking out of his house and going into the ring during a match to help the animals escape. But, he now realized, he'd always felt a sense of security, a belief that it would all work out. Doctors could fix broken bones if you fell off your skateboard. His parents could ground him for sneaking out, but he still had a room full of gadgets and virtual games. And even in the ring, there were trainers and police nearby if he needed saving. His parents had even been able to pay to keep him out of a detention center when he and Leesa had been caught. Now, though, there was no safety net.

Bruce was in the hospital, and even if the mayor brought him back, she was going to force him to perform experiments on them. Marcus's mom had no idea where he was. And he'd been watching Unnaturals matches long enough to know that mutations could cause strange shifts in personality, not to mention the obvious physical changes. Plus, the mutations were, you know, permanent.

"What does it feel like?" Marcus asked, turning his head to look at Francine. The lizard's strange human eyes blinked at him from inside her green face.

"Being the mayor's daughter?" she asked. It was clearly a question she'd been getting all her life.

"No. . . . The, um, *change*."

"Oh, that. Awful! Like your insides are being pulled apart and glued back together."

"Awesome," Leesa said from the bed on the other side

of Francine. "Thanks for the pep talk."

"But afterward, it's not so bad," Francine added quickly, flicking her tongue. "You get used to it. Adapt, I guess. At least I can go outside. I really missed seeing the sun. Actually, to tell you the truth, my life is a lot better as a lizard than it was before."

Okay, now she was just going overboard.

"It'll be worse for us, anyway," Joni whispered. Her voice was hoarse, like she'd been holding in the tears. "You heard the mayor. They're going to experiment on us again and again until they get it right. We're going to be like Laringo."

"Laringo was actually really nice," Francine said. "He was my mom's pet growing up, and he'd always trot over to my hoverchair and lick my face."

"What about now, after he's been given serum after serum?" Joni asked.

Francine's silence said it all.

"What are we going to do?" Marcus asked. The words came out as more of a wail. He was starting to feel really hot, awfully constricted. He pushed against the straps, but they just seemed to tighten around his arms and legs with each movement. The suckers pulled at his skin and the machines beeped in his ears and his breath was coming faster and faster.

Strangely, Leesa was calm. "We're never going to get out of here," Leesa said flatly, as if she'd been expecting this all along. As if she'd known that one day, her bad luck would lead her to this room.

Marcus heaved a huge, dejected sigh and stopped straining. And as soon as he'd stopped making so much noise, he heard something.

The handle of the door was rattling.

Everyone looked toward the door with wide eyes, and Joni called out in a high, thin voice, "Who's there?"

There was a second of silence, and then the door slammed open with such force that it banged into the wall. Mutant animals burst into the small space, and the kids started screaming, sure they were about to be torn to shreds. All except Francine.

"It's okay," she said. "They're my friends."

"Your *friends*?" Leesa asked.

"At least they were. I'm not sure they like me anymore. Hi, Kozmo," Francine called to a fox with bat wings that was whirring around the fluorescent lights. "Hey, Runt!" she giggled as a German shepherd mutt bounded in and started licking her face.

"It's the Swift!" Marcus said, as the other mutants

entered the room. "And the Fearless!" he shouted, seeing the limping grizzly-tiger. Then the eagle-dog trotted in and sniffed his hand, whining, and Marcus thought his heart would burst.

The Fearless snapped Leesa's binds with her sharp saber teeth while the Enforcer pulled at Joni's straps with his eight-tentacled trunks. They were all free in no time.

"Pete!" Marcus burst from H-Ward and rushed over to his brother, who was still leaning against a mop in the middle of the room, despite the stampede and everything.

When Pete was still unresponsive, Marcus started to cry. He didn't even care that Leesa and Joni were watching. His brother was forever changed, and it was all Marcus's fault.

Overhead, the fox-bat screeched. "Kozmo says he's just tranquilized," Francine said. "The Yellow Six give tranquilizers to animals before they run tests."

"You can understand them?" Leesa asked. There was awe in her voice. "That is so cool."

Francine smiled shyly. "She's bringing you the antidote."

They watched as the fox-bat swooped low over the lab tables and snatched up a vial in her jaws, dropping it in Marcus's hand. Marcus looked down at the serum doubtfully, but what choice did he have? As Joni tilted Pete's head back, Marcus dumped the liquid down his brother's throat. In less than a minute, the light had returned to Pete's eyes.

"What's going on?" he asked, blinking.

"Oh, Pete!" Joni said, and planted a big kiss on his lips right in front of all of them.

Marcus involuntarily looked at Leesa, and she blushed and averted her gaze. Now he felt like a real dork. "We have to get out of here," he said, hoping to break up his brother's little smooch session.

"We can't just leave Francine," Leesa said, surprising him. She'd been hostile to the mayor's reptilian daughter at first, but now she seemed to have a kinship with her. Francine was hanging back by H-Ward with the dog, Runt, and both looked uncertain, like they didn't want to leave each other's sides.

"Come with us!" Marcus said.

"My mom will find me." She shifted her stance. "I know how she seems. But she really does mean well. I've heard her and Bruce talking, and they did hope to save the world. I mean, how amazing would it be if we could all go outside again, without fear of being poisoned?"

"And the people of the Drain could finally move aboveground," Leesa said wistfully. They all knew how desperate Drainos were to get out of the tunnels.

"Even if we leave, they'll bring in new kids from the Drain to test on," Marcus pointed out. "You heard Mayor Eris. There's already a waitlist. Soon they'll all look like . . ." He trailed off. Everyone knew what he meant. *They'd look like Francine. Or Antonio.* Which was probably not what they'd signed up for.

Then Leesa's eyes locked with his, and Marcus could see them brighten as if an idea was suddenly taking shape—as if all the clues had finally clicked. "What if we could find the key to the right serum?"

Joni laughed, as if Leesa were joking. After so many years of adult scientists plugging away, what made some kid think she could suddenly solve the problem? But Marcus trusted Leesa more than anyone, and he knew she was serious.

"What do you mean, Lees?" he asked.

"That's a fox-bat," she said, pointing to the creature Francine had called "Kozmo." The animals were sitting off to the side near the empty cages, watching them carefully. Kozmo huddled closer to the eagle-dog as if she knew they were talking about her. "So that's what is in Bruce's notes, right? The thing he goes on and on about being so special? *Vulpes* . . ."

"*Vulpes pongo chiroptera.*" Marcus nodded.

"Right. K-group. And that's what Pete heard the scientists talking about. K-group is the key to everything. Bruce believed that if K-group had survived, he could've found the solution a long time ago."

"Right, but you're not Bruce," Francine cut in. "No offense, but I don't think having the key means much if you're not a scientific genius."

Marcus saw where Leesa was going with this, though. "Pete is," he said, looking at his brother. "Didn't you always want to save animals from extinction? Now's your chance. You can start with the human race." He pulled Bruce's notebook out of his bag. "It's all in there."

Pete wanted to be done with this, that was clear, but the idea of saving humanity was pretty appealing. He took the notebook from Marcus's hand and sat on one of the lab stools, hunching over the pages. They waited as he read.

After a minute, he sat up straighter. "They spliced the gene," Pete said excitedly. "*Vulpes pongo chiroptera* is different because they spliced the gene with chimpanzee DNA."

"What does that mean?"

"It means the fox-bat is not just a mutant, like the other animals. She was created from scratch in a test tube using *pongo* brain cells. It means she's part primate." The kids were still looking at him blankly. "It means she's *compatible with humans*! I just don't understand why Bruce never tried splicing again. I mean, he tried everything else."

Looking at Francine's scaly skin, that much was clear.

"He thought K-group was the ultimate failed experiment," Joni pointed out. "If he thought they had all died early on, that wouldn't bode well for humans."

"So what do you need to do?" Marcus asked, leaning close to Pete. "Can you make the right serum?"

"I think so. The equations are pretty straightforward. I just need some *Vulpes pongo chiroptera* DNA to mix with a harmless virus that we can give to humans. Since it's H-compatible, it should just deliver the genes we want—the ones that are resistant to the sun and pollution—and leave everything else the same."

"Meaning people will still look like people," Francine said, flicking her forked tongue. She turned around and ran back into H-Ward. They could hear glass clinking as she rummaged through the wall of test tubes. After a minute, she slithered back out, shaking her head. "The K-group blood samples aren't here."

"The only other place it would be is in Bruce's office." Pete sighed. "And there's no way I can get in there, at least not any time soon. With everything that's happened, I'm sure NuFormz is on lockdown."

The fox-bat screeched and started flapping her wings. The Underdog barked, and the rabbit-panther thumped her hind leg—it seemed like they were all having some kind of argument. But one more loud screech from the fox-bat silenced the group.

"What about if you took another sample?" Francine said.

The group looked at her questioningly.

"Kozmo says that no one should have to live in a box. That no one should be hidden away underground. That everyone should get to breathe fresh air and feel the sun on their faces—even humans," the lizard-girl explained. "She says you can take her blood sample. Just be gentle."

60

MOST DAYS NOW, THE ROUTINE WAS THE SAME. AFTER school with Ms. Hoiles, Mayor Eris—Eva—would send her private auto-hele to take the kids across the river to the Greenplains.

"Your ride's parked on the beach," Leesa's mom said, walking through the door to their apartment. Ms. Khan was a private consultant for the mayor now, advising on ethical public policy, so she usually just caught the auto-hele down from the sky office to ground level. They still lived in the same apartment in the Drain, but they were saving up, little by little. It was a lot easier now that her mom didn't have to work nights and wasn't so exhausted all the time.

"Great. Let's go, Marcus!" Leesa shut the math textbook and jumped up.

"Homework done?" Ms. Khan asked them.

Marcus nodded. "Leesa just taught me fractions using Unnaturals stats." Ms. Khan raised a questioning eyebrow. "The Mighty is three-fourths zebra. That means he's 25 percent bull."

"And you're only 25 percent spoiled sky kid," Leesa said with a smirk. "Let's go!"

When they landed on the west bank in the Greenplains, Antonio and Francine were there to meet them, like always. But while the tiger-boy and lizard-girl could walk freely in the open air, Leesa and Marcus stayed inside the auto-hele. Its glass sphere detached from the chopper so they could roll along behind their friends, safely protected from the atmosphere.

"Bubble girl," Marcus said, nudging Leesa.

"Hmm?"

"You called me bubble boy when we first met because I was so afraid of getting hurt. Remember? Well, I guess now you're a bubble girl," he teased.

That would change pretty soon, though. Bruce and Pete had taken INVINSIFY through extensive standard lab work. Now that they knew they had the right ingredients, there was no need to test on animals. When they'd finally started the human trials, Bruce had been the first to volunteer. But Mayor Eris insisted she'd try it first—that her citizens couldn't trust her if she wouldn't take the risks for herself.

"The worst that can happen is that I end up like my daughter. And then we'll be a happy little lizard family," she'd joked.

Francine did seem pretty happy. She laughed and leaned into Antonio as they strolled through the forest of the Greenplains in front of the hele-bubble. They chatted with the animals they passed—both mutant kids could understand animal dialects.

"I don't know if I ever really want to try INVINSIFY," Marcus said. "But it would be pretty cool to talk to Castor." They'd learned the eagle-dog's name from Antonio, and they all watched as it soared and dove above them in the clouds, the wind whipping through its shepherd dog fur.

"There's Enza," Antonio called, pointing at the grizzly-tiger lounging on a sunny rock. "And Jazlyn." They watched as the rabbit-panther ran laps on the dirt track circling the field of wildflowers. "And Moss says you should come see Samken in the high-wire performance they're working on for talent show—the octo-elephant will be juggling tomatoes with his tentacled trunks as he balances. Moss swears it's the best act he's ever coached."

Leesa rolled her eyes. Antonio was at peak annoyingness when he was translating for the animals, but still, it was nice to have her friend back. His hard edges had softened, and he was acting a lot less defensive these days. He didn't even seem to mind that he looked like half a tiger and half a boy. She suspected that had a lot to do with Francine.

"I think I just learned how to purr," Antonio announced.

"Really?" Marcus said. "Let's hear it."

"Francine, I think you're *purrrfectly purrrty.*"

Leesa groaned at the corny joke, but Francine was cracking up. She looked at Antonio like he was the most special person she'd ever met. It was clear he felt the same way.

"She really has beautiful eyes. And did you see how she can camouflage her skin to fit in anywhere? So cool!"

Leesa was glad Antonio was spending so much time with Francine. He didn't even seem to mind when Marcus held Leesa's hand when they all strolled through the

Greenplains together. That happened a lot more often lately. Marcus reached for her hand now, and Leesa smiled, giving it a squeeze. He didn't seem to mind her callused palms and chipped nails, and she totally didn't care that his hands got clammy. What she cared about was that little thrill when they first touched, and the way he looked at her shyly, like he was still nervous she wouldn't like him or something.

"I wonder how Joni's book is coming," Marcus said. Joni had been working on a book about the Unnaturals. She was already promoting it on her channel to the Moniacs.

"I don't know how she'll fit everything that's happened in there," Leesa said. "But one thing's for sure: it's one crazy story."